Other books by Shirley Marks:

Geek to Chic
Honeymoon Husband

MISS QUINN'S
QUANDARY

MISS QUINN'S QUANDARY

•

Shirley Marks

AVALON BOOKS
NEW YORK

Sch

Published by Thomas Bouregy & Co., Inc.
160 Madison Avenue, New York, NY 10016

Library of Congress Cataloging-in-Publication Data

Marks, Shirley.
    Miss Quinn's quandary / Shirley Marks.
        p. cm.
    ISBN 978-0-8034-9876-1 (acid-free paper)
    I. Title.

PS3613.A7655M57 2008
813'.6—dc22

                                    2007024230

PRINTED IN THE UNITED STATES OF AMERICA
ON ACID-FREE PAPER
BY HADDON CRAFTSMEN, BLOOMSBURG, PENNSYLVANIA

To Heidi A., who introduced me to Regency England.
Thank you ever so much.

To my darling husband, your love and humor mean
more to me than you can possibly know.
You outrank any earl, duke, or prince!

Chapter One

"Are you quite mad?" Sir Randall Trent thought it a distinct possibility.

The woman whirled and faced him. Her traveling cloak blotted out his world in a blur of forest green and enveloped him with the scent of roses.

"How could you to tell such an outrageous lie?" he continued. "Unless, of course, you are not in full possession of your faculties."

She parted her perfectly formed lips and shushed him. "Do you want someone to hear you?" The bustling of coaches, horses, and voices sounded from the inn yard even though the sun had set. "We're in a comfortable, warm room instead of that drafty old barn with the others, are we not?"

He took a sidelong glance her. No, she wasn't a woman; she was a young lady, and a pretty one at that. "There remains a discrepancy. We are not married to each other as you have claimed."

1

Curly wisps of golden hair escaped from under the bonnet that framed her face. Randall stared into wide, green eyes set above a small, pert nose and an adorable mouth— all of which he found imminently charming. But that was beside the point. What did he expect her to say? Clearly, there was no possible answer that would prove her sanity.

"No one need know," she said, resuming her air of confidence.

"Well, *I* certainly know!" Randall drove an impatient hand through his hair.

"I had to say it," she confessed. "That was the only way I could have stayed in this room." She placed the bandbox she carried on the bed.

I? Didn't she mean *we?* How on earth had he become the lucky one to share this room with this vision of loveliness?

Some guests had traveled to the Blue Boar Inn up the Severn. Many others had arrived from the west by coach. The majority of them were forced to bed down in the stables of the overbooked establishment, an idea Randall would not have looked upon favorably.

Which brought him back to the question: How had he become involved as one member of the fortunate couple to receive the last room at the inn? This young woman had boldly stepped forward and claimed to be a newlywed, choosing him as husband.

"We'll never get away with it. Never." He shook his head. There was a knock at the door.

"Don't look so guilty." She untied the bow, freed the ribbons from under her chin, and removed her bonnet, placing it on the bed. "Why don't you answer the door?"

"What?" Even to his own ears he sounded as if he was suffering from a bout of absentmindedness. The knock sounded again.

"The door," she said, staring wide-eyed at him. "Are you going to open it, or shall I?"

"No. Oh, no. I shall, of course." Randall stumbled toward the door and opened it. One of the inn maids entered with a tray laden with tea, cups, and a small assortment of day-old cakes and stale biscuits.

"Milord, milady," the serving maid said. She dipped a curtsy, set the tray on the low table by the hearth and left without another word.

Sir Randall heard the footsteps fade down the hallway. The inn seemed quieter too. A mixture of jubilant voices and boisterous complaints echoed from the public dining room below.

"Who should ever be the wiser of our circumstance?" the golden-haired beauty continued, flinging off her traveling cloak and laying it next to her discarded bonnet. She walked toward the tea tray and took a seat by the fire. "Tomorrow we shall board the coach and travel to Oxford. The day after, we'll part and never set eyes on one another again. Shall I pour out?"

"What do you mean?" he asked.

"Well, someone must, don't you think? I'm famished." She looked over the scant fare. "Too bad there isn't supper. But I shan't complain." She filled the cups, chose a cake, and proceeded to eat.

"That's not what I meant at all. How do *you* know we'll never see each other again?"

She took a cup of tea and explained. "I am off to spend

the rest of my life with my aunt in Westmoreland. No one in their right mind, given the choice, would live there." She looked at him with an inspecting eye, lingering longer than he felt comfortable. "You appear to me to have a good head upon those strong, broad shoulders."

Randall caught the half smile on her face. His face warmed. Was this chit making him blush? Ridiculous. It was simply the situation. He'd be spending the night alone with this girl. It would make any man uneasy. She might have found herself deep into the thick of things if she had not had the good fortune to stumble upon him. He was a gentleman. He knew *he* could be trusted.

"You're quite right. I won't be headed anywhere near Westmoreland."

"If you don't mind my asking, where is it you are going?"

He didn't mind at all. "To Kent. Far enough from Westmoreland, I should think." Randall tugged on his waistcoat, sat, and took a moment to ponder. "I agree to your plan. But after two days' time, I shall disclaim any knowledge of you. Are we in agreement on this?"

"Completely." She nodded.

"Very well." He lifted a cup and took a sizable swallow of the weak, lukewarm tea. "How shall we handle the sleeping arrangements then?" Randall tried to keep his voice even, as if all this were an everyday occurrence, which it most certainly was not.

"I'm sleeping in the bed. You may sleep wherever you like." She finished the last of the tea and set her cup aside. Her eyes never met his.

"And what if I choose to share your bed?" He felt the

heat of a blush suffuse his face, which did not concern him. The dim lighting would be sufficient to hide his heightened color. "You know nothing about me. I could be a notorious rake, a seducer of innocent maidens." He meant to put a bit of fear into her.

The look in her eyes told him she did not believe a word of it. "Really? Leaving a trail of ruined women behind? I'll have you know I am an excellent judge of character and I can tell you're a gentleman." She took a taper, moved toward the bed, and opened her bandbox. "And, I know your name is Sir Randall Trent, baronet."

"However did you know that?" He thought it unfortunate the surrounding darkness could not mask the surprise in his voice.

"I read the name on the engraved brass plaque on your bag."

He glanced down at his traveling bag. The traitorous plaque gleamed in the firelight.

"I do believe you'll need a pillow, will you not?" She launched one of the bed pillows toward him.

Randall grunted on impact when the pillow hit him square on the back of his head. *Like that, is it?* "I'll just settle on the settee, near the fire." He bit back the impulse to teach this hoyden a lesson she'd not soon forget.

A rustle of fabric and an unrecognizable utterance told Randall the beauty was stripping down to her chemise. He kept his back to her.

"Did you say something?" Still keeping his back to her, he cocked an ear in her direction.

"I asked if you wanted my cloak to cover you. Since you're near the fire, you won't be needing blankets."

He hadn't a chance to answer, for in the next moment Randall found her cloak hanging from his head. He pulled it off and dropped it onto the pillow she had assaulted him with earlier. "How utterly gracious of you."

"Don't mention it," she returned in a sweet, lilting coo. She blew out her candle and slipped into bed. "Good night, Sir Randall."

"Good night . . ." He paused and peered into the darkness. "I don't know who you are."

"My name," she said, "is Miss Larissa Quinn."

Setting her hairbrush on the table next to the bed, she laid her cheek on the cool pillow and kept still, not wanting to draw any attention to herself. Larissa was as far from sleep as she could be. Her heart pounded so very hard. Never in her life had she done anything as outrageous as she had done on this day.

That morning she had left Miss Simmons' Seminary for Young Ladies. It was the first time in all of her eighteen years she had ever been on her own. At the seminary, there was always someone to tell you what to do, how to behave, or when to speak, and she was so very tired of it.

It was that morning, while traveling up the Severn, when she had decided to do something about her wasted life. Something bold, something exciting, something memorable.

Now she shared a room with a perfect stranger. What could be more memorable than that? Troubling second thoughts began to emerge. This was a foolhardy thing to do. She rolled over to one side. She should have acted with more sense. She tossed once again. The rustle of sheets must have told Sir Randall she had not yet drifted off.

"Have you always been like this, Miss Quinn?" he asked.

Larissa ran her hand over the counterpane, smoothing the wrinkles. "Like what?"

"Adventurous and impulsive."

"No. This is the first time." She tried to bolster her normally soft and timid voice.

"Your first, you say? I find that nearly impossible to believe. You seem quite adept at fabricating the wildest of lies and passing them off as truths. That innocent face of yours does not betray the deceitful words your tongue chooses to utter. It could prove most dangerous for a young girl. You come across as quite bold and knowing."

"I'm not really, you know. Most people would describe me as rather shy."

"Shy?"

Larissa could almost swear she heard him chuckle. She sat up in bed and held the top sheet to her throat. There at the foot of her bed, in the illumination of the flickering fire, stood Sir Randall.

Larissa had never seen a man in braces before. She tried not to let the shock of his undress register on her face. His collar lay open and his shirtsleeves were rolled up to his elbows, revealing his gently muscular forearms. His right thumb hooked the waistband of his inexpressibles. The other hand gripped the post of the bed.

She swallowed hard. "I only behaved as I did because I'm afraid of wasting away in the country without ever having experienced life."

"Is it so important?" The light of the flames danced off Sir Randall's profile, displaying his finely formed straight nose and angular jaw.

"Oh, yes. Having every choice made for you, not having to think for yourself, and every day being the same as the next can be very boring. I'm afraid my future doesn't look much brighter. I'm to care for my aged aunt." She was expecting the worst. "I doubt I will ever know what it is like to live."

Sir Randall had moved to the side of her bed. His proximity afforded her the opportunity to take a good, long look at him. Larissa guessed he wasn't much older than she, although she believed he had undoubtedly more worldly experience. She noticed the hint of dark stubble that swept across the lower half of his face and over his upper lip.

"What is there to know?" All he need do was whisper, for he now stood next to the bed.

She stared into his eyes. Dark eyes framed by black arched brows. Eyes black as the night, and strangely comforting, held her captive. Curiosity overcame her fright. "What life is like outside the seminary."

"Life? I take it that also includes men." Sir Randall drew Larissa's hair away from her face with his fingertips and smoothed it back with his hand.

Larissa felt his strong, gentle fingers run through her hair and brush against her chin. His touch left a burning imprint on her flesh. "Men are a complete mystery to me." She luxuriated in his touch, bathed in warmth that emanated from him.

She could see the outline of his torso under the folds of

his shirt. Teasing her from the opening was the gentle slope of the muscles of his chest. He smelled musky, a heady scent that filled her senses.

If she were truly bold, she would not retreat from his unassuming advance. However, no matter how daring she wished to pretend to be, Larissa knew it would be quite beyond her.

"The world can be both a wonderful and a dangerous place, Miss Quinn. I should be very careful if I were you. A young lady just can't go gallivanting about the country-side alone."

"And why not? You're traveling alone."

"I'm a man."

Larissa couldn't prevent a smile from taking her lips. It felt naughty to feel pleasure as she answered, "Yes, I had noticed."

Sir Randall stepped back and returned to his makeshift bed. "Good night, Miss Quinn."

"Good night, Sir Randall." Only when he stepped away did she notice the sheet she had used in modesty to cover herself now lay in her lap.

Chapter Two

Randall rubbed his tormented hands together and gave a tolerant sigh. Most men might take advantage of the situation. He settled back on the settee and drew his booted feet away from the edge. Although sleep continued to elude him, he thought it best to keep his thoughts away from Larissa.

If Larissa had been as shy as she claimed, she must have been making a tremendous effort to change her natural ways. Indeed, Randall admired her conviction and strength in trying to overcome what she considered a weakness.

He pulled her cloak over his shoulder and snuggled it under his chin. The blasted garment smelled of her. Yes, she acted naive. Randall had heard the nervousness in her voice. Every now and then, he saw in her eyes uncertainty, hesitation, and perhaps even a mote of fear.

If he had met her at a social gathering and been properly

introduced by a chaperone, perhaps he would have regarded her in a quite a different light. But meeting her under these unfavorable circumstances nullified any type of relationship. She was pretty, she was interesting, but most of all, she was far too unpredictable for Randall's tastes.

Regardless of her timid or bold nature, her sheltered or unworldly upbringing, Larissa said whatever came to mind, indifferent of the consequences. He knew this type of behavior could lead to nothing but trouble.

He tugged at the traveling cloak. It was growing devilishly hot in here. He rested his head on the padded bolster and forced himself not to look toward the bed.

This situation was impossible. He could not remain. Randall could not stay the night in the same room with this young woman. He pulled himself up into a sitting position, gathered his clothes, and rather than make excuses, left without a word.

It wasn't until Randall had settled into a chair in the dining room that he realized he still had Larissa's cloak. It was a reminder of why he would remain here. He felt thankful that he had her cloak providing warmth for there'd not be much rest for him this night.

The next morning brought the bustle of yard boys, vendors, ostlers, and travel-worn passengers eager to be on their way. The commotion woke Randall. His eyelids were heavy and he rubbed his whisker-stubbled chin. The mild scent of roses from the cloak he held near his face reminded him of his circumstance and he thought of Larissa. How had she fared alone in their room?

He eased out of his chair and climbed the stairs to look

in on her. He rapped softly on the door with his knuckle and waited. The door creaked open; there in the dim morning light stood Larissa, washed, dressed, and ready to leave.

"What time did you get up?" Randall croaked. His throat was dry and he had a kink in his neck.

Larissa opened the door, allowing him to enter the room. "About an hour ago, before the sun rose. I am accustomed to rising at that time."

Randall groaned. He wasn't used to getting up much before noon.

"I'll go to the public dining room for some tea."

"That's a good idea." He smiled. This would give him an opportunity for his morning toilette without her underfoot. "I'll join you presently. Thank you for the use of your cloak." He returned her garment.

Larissa slung it over her arm. "I thank you for indulging me." She took up her reticule and bandbox and left.

Randall helped Larissa into the coach and followed her in. She settled in the window seat closest to the door on the left. Down the bench in the farthest corner, a well-dressed man, who looked very out of place in a public transport, reeked of stale spirits and lay limp against the inside of the coach. On the opposite side, a rotund couple took up the entire bench. Randall had no choice but to sit next to Larissa.

"Ah, Miss Quinn, lovely to see you again," the plump woman greeted. "Good morning." She raised her hand to her round, flushing cheek. "I suppose I should say, Mrs. Quinn—and to you also, Mr. Quinn."

Mr. Quinn? Randall's breath caught in his throat. Why had she called him that?

With a nod, Mr. Briggs only grunted, echoing his wife's sentiments.

"This is Mr. and Mrs. Briggs. I met them as we traveled up the Severn yesterday," Larissa explained.

Randall touched the brim of his hat and nodded. He understood. Mrs. Briggs had met Larissa Quinn yesterday and must have supposed that he, being apparently married to her, must make him Mr. Quinn.

The courtyard horn sounded and the stagecoach lurched into motion, pulling out of the inn yard and leaving behind the noises of the throng. The wheels dropped into the well-rutted road and it took only a few moments for the transport to gain its traveling pace. The coach fell into its familiar rocking rhythm. The only sounds remaining were the jingling of harnesses and the horses' clipping hooves.

"It's very strange." Mrs. Briggs' eyes narrowed, giving Randall a rather lengthy inspection. "I don't recall seeing your husband yesterday."

"My poor darling. He was hanging over the railing the entire time," Larissa explained. "Water travel doesn't agree with him."

"A tragedy, Mr. Quinn," Mrs. Briggs offered, in what she probably considered a sympathetic tone.

"Thank you," he said and offered a practiced, friendly smile. He feared it was going be a long trip.

"Where is your maid, dear?" Mrs. Briggs had clasped her hands in front of her, while her face reflected a multitude of concerns.

"I am without one," Larissa said, giving a demure lowering of her lashes. Her adorable mouth curved into an exquisite moue. "Mr. Quinn doesn't see me a fit lady."

Randall gasped. Why on earth did she have to say that?

Mrs. Briggs puffed up, her hands tightened into two small, hard fists. "An unfit lady? I'll show you an unfit lady, melord!" Her knuckles were turning white. "Why, Mrs. Quinn is *the* most—"

Randall nearly choked on his breath. "You misunderstand my . . . my . . . my wife," he stammered. "What she means to say is, at the moment we cannot afford such an extravagance. We have just returned from our voyage and all. We have not as of yet even settled into a home. We haven't hired anyone." He flashed a smile, one he hoped would dissuade her from the violence he imagined she might inflict were her anger unleashed.

Randall thought Mr. Briggs looked well cowed, a fate he would wish to avoid at all costs. "Believe me, there is no one in the world like my Larissa." Which was the absolute truth. With an incline of his head, he brought their heads together so they just touched in what he thought was a show of affection.

"Ain't that sweet?" Mrs. Briggs sighed. "Now, don't you two make a lovely couple?"

Randall rolled his eyes toward Larissa, who gave a silly smile in return. One of adoration, he supposed. It was enough to silence Mrs. Briggs for the moment.

Mr. Briggs finally succumbed to the motion of the vehicle and dozed off. Randall watched Mrs. Briggs' wandering eyes make a careful inspection, first over Larissa, then over him.

"You haven't said a word to one another since we've left," she said. Against Randall's fervent hopes, Mrs. Briggs continued, "Have you had a spat? Lover's quarrel already?"

"We've hit a bit of a rough spot, you might say," Randall said in a confidential whisper to Mrs. Briggs and glanced back at Larissa, who to his amazement remained silent.

"That'll never do." Mrs. Briggs moved to the edge of her seat, closer to the couple. "If you don't patch your quarrel now, you're bound to end up like me and the mister." Their attention momentarily shifted to Mr. Briggs, snoring away in the corner of the rocking coach. It wasn't a pleasant sight.

Randall had to agree. One wouldn't want to turn out like that. He certainly didn't.

"Please, Mr. Quinn, say you're sorry and give your bride a kiss."

Randall looked from Mrs. Briggs to Larissa, who both stared back at him. He knew the type. Mrs. Briggs would never relent. He might as well submit.

Randall looked to Larissa again. She batted her long, thick lashes and gave a cherubic smile. Blast her, she was enjoying it all. He murmured a halfhearted "Sorry," and brushed his lips against her cheek.

"Aggh, no! That's a kiss you give your grandmother," Mrs. Briggs scolded. "Look at her, man. She's a beautiful girl! She's your wife! Mr. Quinn, give her a husbandly kiss."

He glanced over to Larissa again. She still wore that inviting smile. Randall saw her wink, goading him. He decided Larissa could use a sound kissing. Now he had his chance to shock some sensibility into her. At the same time, he'd certainly give Mrs. Briggs an eyeful and good cause to cease her meddling ways.

"You don't want to spend another minute in anger. Go on, Mr. Quinn."

All in full view of Mrs. Briggs, who sat front row center, Randall took action. He drew Larissa to him and gazed into her green eyes and uttered, "My darling, I'm terribly sorry for any discomfort I have caused you. You were right and I was wrong." That would about cover the apology gamut.

Randall descended, covering Larissa's soft lips with his own. The same sweet scent that lingered on Larissa's cloak keeping him warm the night before rushed through his head.

With a shriek, Mrs. Briggs' eyes bugged out in shock at the public display.

Randall ended the kiss and gave his solemn vow, "Dear heart, henceforth I shall do my utmost never to quarrel with you again."

With a final cry, Mrs. Briggs rolled her eyes toward the heavens. A bout of the vapors overcame her and she fell into a heap against the cushions.

Satisfied with the reaction, Randall settled the limp Larissa back into her seat. She sat without saying a word, without the slightest movement and with her eyes wide as saucers.

Randall was quite pleased with the results. That would show the pair of them. He snugged his hat low on his forehead and spent the remainder of his trip in relative peace and quiet. Only the snores of Mrs. Briggs could be heard drowning out the wheezing of Mr. Briggs.

Sleep came easily for Randall after conversation in the coach ceased. But he soon woke to the pungent scent of roses and a weight leaning on his right arm. He forced his eyes open only to notice a slumbering Larissa snug and comfortable, holding his arm firmly with both hands. Her leg pressed tightly against his and her angelic face tilted upward.

A quick glance around told Randall the passengers all slept. "Miss Quinn," he whispered. "Miss Quinn, wake up." He took a second look to see if he had disturbed anyone. He moved his shoulder, trying to rouse her with no success. He did manage to stir her, only to have her wrap her hands more tightly about his arm and snuggle closer to him.

Chapter Three

Some hours later when Larissa awoke, she straightened from her semi-reclining position against the side of the coach and looked around. The nameless man in the corner still slept. Mr. and Mrs. Briggs across from her took turns punctuating the silence with their snores.

Larissa allowed herself to stare at the dozing Sir Randall. His head was tipped back and delicately balanced as he slept. Even after hours of travel, his dark, curly hair was still sculpted to perfection. His fingers were locked onto the brim of his hat, which rested on his lap, and his legs were crossed at the ankles, resting between Mr. and Mrs. Briggs.

Although she had not seen many men up close, she knew he certainly must be one of the most handsome. The memory of Sir Randall's kiss was fresh in her mind. While she slept, she had replayed the moment over and over in her dreams, feeling the strong hold of his arms as he drew her down to his lap, the taut muscles of his thighs hard against her back and the spreading warmth in the places where their bodies touched.

So that was what it felt like to be kissed by a man. It was magnificent.

The thought alone sent the blood coursing through her. She had felt both frightened and exhilarated. Never had she felt so alive as at the moment his well-formed lips pressed against hers. She began to feel dizzy, whether from remembered sensation or lack of air she wasn't sure. He had borne down on her, pressing her into his lap.

The stagecoach drew to a halt at the White Horse Inn and the passengers disembarked. Mrs. Briggs did not wait for Mr. Briggs, but made a quick escape from the confines of the coach. Not to stretch her legs, but to escape the company of the pervert Mr. Quinn.

A smug smile crossed Randall's face. The more he thought about the incident, the less shocking he thought it, and the more he enjoyed it. He knew Mrs. Briggs would never, ever speak to him again. That alone brought about the greatest satisfaction he could have imagined.

Randall followed Mr. Briggs and reached in for Larissa to help her down. "My dear."

"Thank you, Sir Randall," she murmured, taking his proffered hand. Her eyes did not meet his and he noticed the heightened color on her face. In his high humor, he had not considered her innocence.

In the dark interior of the coach Randall caught the movement of the remaining passenger and an unexplained flash. Was it a reflection of some type? Whoever the man was, he had slept the entire way and not made a sound.

But who could have heard any conversation over the resonant snores of the Briggs?

Randall tucked Larissa's hand in the crook of his arm, escorting her inside.

"Two rooms, please," he said to the innkeeper. Randall scrawled in the register. He did not say whether this girl on his arm was his sister, wife, or paramour. Nor did the innkeeper ask. Randall had no intention of perpetuating the marriage lie they had so thoughtlessly originated.

"Betty!" the innkeeper shouted. "Take Mr. Trent and"—he squinted at the following line in the book—"the lady up to their rooms."

Betty, a young servant clad in near rags, darted out from the next room. "This way, your lordship." She dipped curtsy and led Randall and Larissa to their rooms on the second floor.

Betty swung open one door. "I 'ope you'll be likin' this room, ma'am."

Larissa stepped inside, nodded in approval and thanked her softly. Betty passed by Randall and opened another door.

"This is your room, your lordship."

A quick inspection told him the bed was not large, but clean enough. He would welcome a good night's sleep after spending the previous night at a table, resting against a wall.

"Will that be all, your lordship?"

"We will want to supper in our rooms."

"Right away, your lordship." Betty bobbed a curtsy and dashed down the hall.

Randall stood in the doorway feeling torn as to whether

he should check to see if Larissa was properly settled, or respect her privacy. The decision was instantaneously made for him by the arrival of the innkeeper followed by a well-dressed man.

The innkeeper opened the door to the room on the other side of Randall's. For the briefest of moments, the well-dressed man's searching gaze met Randall's. In the dim light, he saw the reflection of the gold-capped front tooth from the man's wide grin.

Randall stepped into his room and closed the door. That man. Certainly it was the same man from the coach. He made Randall feel exceedingly uncomfortable. That gold tooth blinked like an all-seeing, all-knowing eye. He knew the man could not have known what took place in the coach. The man's liquored state had seen to that, hadn't it? The man could only have recognized him as someone who had disembarked from the coach.

Randall stretched out on the bed and draped his arm over his tired eyes. From now on, he would mind his own business and he hoped everyone else would do the same.

The latch made a soft click when Larissa closed the door. She laid her bandbox on the bed and removed her bonnet before opening her reticule and pulling out the letter from Aunt Ivy. Her eyes scanned the shaky scrawl. Her aunt must be quite old. The phrases that stood out were "you can help fill my days," "it has been so long since I have had promise of such delightful company," and "a companion to stead me through my declining years."

It didn't sound promising. Perhaps growing up in the confines of the seminary had prepared her for the rigorous days ahead. How sweet dear Aunt Ivy had been to offer her a place to live. Larissa was grateful. She would do what she could to make an old woman's last years comfortable. Larissa had little medical experience to draw from. Small burns, cuts, and wounds she could manage, but caring for the infirm and aged, she thought, might be beyond her.

Larissa realized she might have to face those years without making any acquaintances of another man, but not without a memory. She had memories that would last—Sir Randall and his—their kiss. She could dream of him night after night. Not that she had much choice, for he had made his imprint on her mind. He was the first thought she had when she awoke, and the last lingering image before she fell asleep. How could she ever forget him?

Randall's room overlooked the inn's courtyard. He watched Mr. and Mrs. Briggs step into another transport several hours later. Who knew when the other man would leave? That man was of no concern; he had been asleep and had heard nothing.

He could look forward to leaving Mrs. Briggs, the man with the gold tooth, and Miss Larissa Quinn behind. After tonight, he would never give the lot of them another thought. Tomorrow, life would return to normal.

He'd stay out of the public dining room. He'd asked for a supper of meat pies, vegetables, and two tankards of porter to be brought up for dinner. Randall removed a tankard and a pie for himself and would deliver the second plate next door to Larissa.

Thinking of that man with a golden tooth caused Randall

to pause in his room with his hand motionless on the door latch. He shrugged the thought aside, opened the door, and stepped into the hall. A quick glance around the empty corridor made him feel more at ease. When he rapped on Larissa's door, she was quick to answer and he was equally as quick to step inside.

Larissa's room smelled fresh, but not from her refreshing presence, as Randall first thought. She had opened the window, allowing the air to circulate.

"I've brought you supper, Miss Quinn." Randall set the tray on the table. "I think it best if we avoid the public dining room."

"I'm sure you know best in these matters. Thank you." She kept a respectable distance between them.

Randall had not realized how much of a schoolgirl she was, especially with her hair let down. How could she have changed from the teasing chit in the coach who taunted him into kissing her to this innocent?

"I'll be leaving at dawn," he added. "You'll be safe if you stay in your room until it's time to board your transport." Why did he continue to feel responsible for her?

"I thank you for your concern," she said in not much more than a whisper. She hugged her book tightly to her chest.

Was she frightened of him? Did she think he would do what he did on the coach? Or worse, perhaps? He wanted to reassure her that he had no such intention. Then, just as quickly, he changed his mind, thinking it was not necessary. It was best he leave.

Randall opened the door, then turned back to Larissa. Her green eyes stared up at him.

"In the future, I think it best if you ask who is on the other side of the door before allowing them in." A smile washed over his face. One he hoped would relay warmth and kindness. Opening the door, Randall's first glimpse outside the room was the flash of gold. He hurried to his room and closed the door behind him. He could not fathom why he found that man so disturbing.

A few hours later, Randall lay awake staring at the wall. He knew that just on the other side of that wall lay Larissa.

The sole niggling regret he had experienced upon the accomplishment of his minor indiscretion now blossomed into a tumult of doubt and self-recrimination. Guilt racked his brain, leaving him unable to sleep. Now he felt certain that the instant when their lips met, it had been the first time she had been kissed. He was leading an innocent astray.

That was likely why he couldn't get her off his mind—he felt guilty. It was no wonder he tossed in bed. He would never see Larissa again and his conscience would not let him rest. He would have to make amends for his actions while he had the chance.

Randall ignored the lateness of the hour, drew on his trousers and slipped into his shirt. In bare feet, he tiptoed out his door to Larissa's room.

He knocked softly while drawing one of his braces onto his shoulder.

"Who is it?" came her answer.

"It's me, Randall, of course," he replied. A smile lit on his lips knowing she had taken his suggestion and was showing some caution.

The door slid open, revealing Larissa's eye and a corner of her mouth. He shot quick glances down either side of the hallway looking for any sign of observers.

"Quick, let me in," he urged. With that he pushed the door open and stepped inside. But not before someone rounded the far corner of the hallway. Before Randall could close the door, he saw the glimmer of gold as the man gave a lewd smile and winked at him.

In the absence of a wrapper, Larissa had thrown on her green traveling cloak to admit Sir Randall into her room. He swept in and latched the door behind him.

"I'm sorry to disturb you at this hour," he said, more concerned with the man in the hallway than the woman in the room.

Larissa was glad, even excited, to see him. Especially in this state of undress. Bootless, no less. She actually preferred Sir Randall this way. He was less stuffy, less arrogant, less covered. He was all she dreamed of last night and all she wished for today. It pleased her to see how well she had remembered the planes of his face and the angle of his jaw, the arch of his dark brow and the gentle intensity in his eyes.

"There's something I need to say." He didn't even look at her. Was she all that dreadful in her green traveling cloak? "What I did in the coach. When . . . I . . . kissed you." He ran his hands through his hair. "Well, I only want to apologize. I'm frightfully sorry." He sounded remorseful. "It was very heartless of me to do such a thing."

It was the single most exciting thing in her dreary life. How could he say he was sorry?

"I wouldn't blame you if you thought ill of me." Her

gaze followed his thumb as it ran under his brace from his shoulder along his well-formed chest to the waistband of his inexpressibles.

"I told you, Sir Randall. I am a very good judge of character. You have nothing to be ashamed of." Larissa admitted, "I, too, have regrets about my actions."

"Ah, yes," he sighed and finally met her eyes. "The 'We're married! Give us the last room' incident."

"If you hadn't flirted so shamelessly on the ship, I would never have suggested it."

"Shameless flirting?" A confused look crossed his face. He had tipped his hat and wished her a good day. "I was merely being polite."

"Well, when one comes from a ladies' seminary, one isn't accustomed to such behavior from a gentleman."

Randall felt the same unsettled confusion as when he spoke with his Uncle Cyrus. "Coming from a ladies' seminary, one wouldn't be accustomed to men at all."

"My point exactly." Larissa punctuated her statement with the nod of her head.

It *was* like speaking to his Uncle Cyrus. It was best just to end the discussion. He had apologized, and it seemed to him no harm was done. "Good night, Miss Quinn, and goodbye." With as formal a bow as one could perform in one's shirtsleeves and stocking feet, he left.

Larissa watched Sir Randall make his retreat. With a distinct click of the door handle, he was gone. She removed her cloak, dropped it onto the bed and crawled under the covers.

She would remember him for as long as she lived. She would dream about him in the dreary days, months, and years that followed. Perhaps she even loved him, just a little, for he was the first man to kiss her. It was a moment she would hold in her heart forever.

She had hoped he had come to kiss her goodbye. It was far more than she could wish. It was more likely she would never lay her eyes or her lips upon him again.

Chapter Four

Randall's hired hackney rolled up the long, winding cobblestone drive leading to Rushton Manor. Randall sat quietly, still weary from the trip from The Blue Boar to the White Horse in Oxford. It had been two days and thoughts of Larissa Quinn were only beginning to ebb. During the day he busied himself, but at night she would come to him in his dreams.

Larissa's angelic face peering through the long, loose blond hair tumbling about her shoulders, falling almost to her waist. The image lacked color as it had that memorable night in the darkened room. In his vivid recollections he thought of her voice as soft and low as she called to him. Why could he not forget her?

Sleep was a luxury these days. By the end of the week, even tonight perhaps, he would return to a night of normal sleep. He could count on an interesting, if not somewhat unusual evening spent in his Uncle Cyrus' company. That would be all that was needed to remove thoughts of Larissa from his mind.

The coach stopped in front of the looming Tudor and Randall disembarked. He approached the great double oak doors and knocked. He could easily study the intricate carvings of the fifteenth-century doors for an extended period of time. One had no choice but to examine the detail because it took an extraordinarily long time for the butler, Watkins, to admit awaiting guests—if Watkins still held the post of butler.

Watkins was old during Randall's last visit three years ago and barely mobile then. As Randall stood pondering the possibilities, he hardly noticed the lengthy stretch of time creep by before the massive front door began to inch open.

Randall leaned toward the small opening, finding it wasn't large enough to squeeze through yet. He felt torn as to whether he need help Watkins with the front door or not. If the butler was ancient before, the man must be near the age of Methuselah now. He was slow as treacle in the dead of winter and as fragile as fine bone porcelain, but to Randall's amazement the elderly butler still thrived.

Randall stepped inside as soon as the space between the doors allowed his entry.

"Good day, Watkins."

"Yes, sir," is all the butler said.

"Is my uncle about?"

"If I were you, sir, I would not be speakin' 'bout his lordship in those terms."

The butler's response bewildered Randall long enough

for the ringing of heels on the marble floor to announce the Earl of Rushton.

"Welcome, my boy! Welcome!" He took Randall's hand and pumped it with vigor. Rushton clapped his nephew on the back. "Let me take a good look at you." Rushton circled him like a vulture. "You're looking well, very well indeed." He examined the cut of his coat, the fit of his breeches, and the intricate folds of his cravat.

"Will there be anything else you require, your lordship?" Watkins gave the appearance of always being on the verge of tottering over and Randall kept on guard to catch him.

"We'll have port in the library," Rushton ordered.

"Very well, my lord," Watkins answered and shuffled off down the hallway.

"Would have thought Watkins dead by now, Uncle, or at least retired." Randall watched the butler disappear into the library.

Rushton shook his finger at his nephew. "Don't be disrespectful, boy." He gave Randall a push, starting him toward the library. "He was butler for my father, and his father before him."

"It wouldn't surprise me at all, to find he worked for the first Earl of Rushton," Randall snorted, just before stepping into the library.

"Not so loud, lad. Watkins will hear you."

Randall spun to face his uncle. "Hear me? He can still hear?"

"Yes, sir. Thank you for asking," the butler responded. "And the wife still resides here also."

Between his uncle's ramblings and the butler's questionable interpretation, conversation must be interesting around the manor, Randall thought.

Rushton motioned to the wingback chairs in front of the blazing hearth and they sat. "Now tell me, how was your trip?" He closed one eye and gave a measuring glare. "You seem a bit frayed around the edges."

"Well, it was long and troublesome. Nothing I'd want to relate. Would rather put it all behind me, really."

"Good! Good!" Uncle Cyrus praised in a fevered pitch. Watkins had insinuated himself between them and proffered a tray with two glasses. Rushton took one glass. "I shall have my valet speak to you at once. You look bang up to the mark, dressed in the first stare of fashion and all that."

"What's the urgency?" Randall asked, taking the remaining glass. Although his uncle was somewhat unpredictable, he always had a reason for his actions. Not necessarily good ones, but Randall was becoming increasingly curious.

"I've called you here so you could accompany me." Rushton took a swallow of port and his eyes grew large with excitement. "We're off to London."

"London? Whatever for?" The news did not please Randall.

"I've come to the conclusion it's high time I remarry," Rushton announced. "Don't you think?"

Randall tried his best to hide his amused smile and gazed into his glass. "Well, I really can't speak for you, Uncle."

"Of course not!" Rushton bellowed. "Wouldn't permit it. Would be demmed pretentious of you. But I'm not getting any younger, you know." He patted his rounded belly and grazed his hand over the scant hair covering his head. "Haven't got the looks you have, what?" It had occurred to Randall if they had been related by blood and not by marriage, they might have looked more similar. "But a man needs companionship in his advancing years. And the comfort of a woman every now and again, even at my age."

"If you say so, sir." It was becoming an increasingly difficult task for Randall to keep his laughter reined.

"Of course I say so," Uncle Cyrus blustered. "My wealth and my title are my best features, I'll wager. But make no mistake, I'll still have my pick." He set aside his glass and stood. "Stand up, let's have another look at you, boy."

Randall did as requested. His uncle rotated him slowly to have a good look at the back of his coat. Completing the turn, Randall could not help but notice his uncle staring at the dark curls that graced Randall's head.

"I do admire those curls of yours."

Randall got the distinct impression it was not the curls that drew his uncle's admiration, it was the amount of hair, plain and simple. Uncle Cyrus hadn't any to spare, another reason to keep Watkins around as butler. He was the only one who had less hair than Randall's uncle.

Uncle Cyrus had tried to create the illusion of a pompadour by pulling his long strands of hair from the sides of his head and curling them around on the top like a braided rug, plastering the mass down with a mixture of sugar, glycerin, and water. It wasn't in Randall's nature to stare at the phenomenon, but one couldn't help but have one's eyes drawn to the elaborate, manmade configuration.

"Uncle Cyrus, you make yourself sound positively ancient."

"We won't be a pair of young bucks waltzing into Almack's. I'm counting on your dashing good looks to draw the beauties, while I do the pretty." He sketched a practice bow for his nephew's consideration. "Still, I think I can always use a few pointers, don't you?" He leaned over and caught the hem of Randall's brocade waistcoat between his fingers and felt the fabric. "Nice, yes, very nice. I'll need a new wardrobe and maybe a . . ." He sucked in his gut and gave his slightly protruding midsection a pat.

"Corset? Good heavens, no, Uncle," Randall gasped. "Those things look so demmed silly. You'll be all red in the face and go about creaking. People will talk behind your back about what a trussed-up ass you are."

"The Regent wears one, if I'm not mistaken," Rushton stated with a haughty air.

"No one said Prinny was fashionable. No one dares say it to his face, anyway." Randall sat in his chair and took up his glass. "If he were not a prince, how many ladies would be after him, corset or no?"

"You're quite right. I'm an earl. I don't need a corset." Rushton returned to his seat, retrieving his drink. "You don't suppose someone would marry me just for me, do you?"

Randall gave a smile. "I don't see why not. You're a fine man, any woman should consider herself lucky to have you."

"Thank you, my boy." Rushton sat back in his chair. He raised his glass toward his nephew in appreciation. "I knew there was a good reason I took a liking to you. I hope you're up to traveling. I've told my valet we are to leave in two days' time." Randall did not have a chance to give an answer. "When I was your age, I'd be ready at a moment's notice, and could travel all night if need be."

"I shall be ready, Uncle," Randall offered. "Who else will accompany us?"

"I'll need Georges, of course. A good valet will prove indispensable once my new wardrobe is assembled."

Randall hid his smile. He wondered exactly when it was his uncle had become a slave to fashion. "Will Watkins be with us as well?"

"I'm afraid not." Rushton glanced about for the butler. "He's better off left in the country." He leaned closer to his nephew. "I'm afraid his Portman Square days are over. He's not able to manage the stairs, you know."

Randall nodded, understanding. As he recalled there were three flights of stairs in the townhouse. In the butler's present tottering condition he would have a time of it legging it up and down a single set.

"Once we arrive our first stop will be the tailor."

"Weston is said to be the best."

Rushton held his hand up. "Weston's it is, then. We will need boots, hats, gloves—" The earl stopped and gazed beyond Randall.

Unsure if his uncle was actually looking *at* something, or someone, Randall took a quick glance over his shoulder. There was nothing there.

"A new walking stick or two might be in order, also. And of course a betrothal ring."

"Betrothal ring?" Randall sat forward. "Isn't that a bit premature?"

"Might meet her that first night. Must be ready."

"But, Uncle, really!" All this elaborate planning for a lady—a lady whose identity he did not even know. But Randall knew, with his uncle's uncompromising nature, it was only a matter of time before they discovered who the lucky lady would be.

Chapter Five

The motion and bumps of the transport did not distract Larissa from disquieting thoughts of her aunt. Her father had never spoken of his elder sister at any length. His was not a bitter silence but a sad one, as if he did not want to bring up any unpleasant memories. Then, nearly a year after his death, Larissa had received a letter from her remaining long-lost relative, offering her a home.

Larissa did not have much say in the matter; Miss Simmons was only too glad to respond favorably and wished her ex-pupil good luck. Larissa felt a bit apprehensive of the opportunity at first—she knew nothing of the outside world, not to mention the entire situation regarding her aunt. Was she in a bad state? Confined to her room? An invalid perhaps? Larissa imagined her aunt's home as a small, dimly-lit, dingy country hovel, making the seminary years feel luxurious in comparison.

Even now her Aunt Ivy must have help of some type

considering her frail condition. Larissa hoped the kind woman who helped her aunt would continue to help, admitting that two pairs of hands would ease the burden for her.

The rented hack drew to a halt in front of her aunt's house. Holding the strings of her reticule with both hands, Larissa drew a deep breath, fortifying herself before facing what daunting tasks lay ahead.

She disembarked then froze, staring at the house before her. This wasn't what she expected at all. The residence appeared not large in size but grand. Brick walls and venetian windows faced her on this side of the modest stately country home.

She approached the front door and used the brass dolphin-shaped knocker. An impeccably dressed, statuesque butler answered the door. Larissa would have never guessed her aunt would be able to employ several servants.

"I am Miss Quinn. I believe my aunt is expecting me."

The butler stepped back, without uttering a word, and opened the door wide. Larissa stepped through the portal. Wood paneling surrounded her in the foyer, and a wide staircase spiraled up to the right. Larissa was amazed at the richly appointed interior. This was far beyond what she had expected.

Two recessed alcoves flanked the set of double doors at the far end of the entry hall. In each alcove, a columned pedestal held a statue. On the right was Artemis bathing and on the left Actaeon in mid-transformation, half man, half stag.

Her visual tour stopped at the sight of three large trunks stacked in the foyer.

Did she have the wrong house? It appeared the occupants were readying themselves to leave, and she had only just arrived.

The rustle of taffeta skirts and staccato steps announced the lady of the house. "Oh, it's you, Larissa, my dear girl!" the woman squealed. "My dear, dear, dear girl." She took Larissa into her arms and gave a squeeze, making it difficult for Larissa's lungs to hold air.

Was this her *aged* aunt?

"I'm your Aunt Ivy. Now, let me have a look at you, my dear." She held Larissa out at arm's length, a great, welcoming smile on her kind face. "You look so much like him. Your father, that is. He was such a wonderful man." Tears came to Ivy's eyes. "I am sorry to keep you standing about like this after your long trip. Do come in." She drew Larissa into the foyer. "Hayes, take care of my niece's luggage."

"At once, my lady."

"Let us go into the drawing room and have some tea," she murmured to Larissa. "Hayes, tea and biscuits, please. Or would you care to have something more to eat?" Larissa opened her mouth to speak but hadn't a chance to answer. "How thoughtless of me, of course you would. Hayes, have cook send a plate to keep Larissa until dinner."

"At once, my lady."

This was not what Larissa had expected. Not only was her aunt *not* aged, she seemed teeming with more enthusiasm than Larissa had ever seen contained in a single human being. Her aunt, it was now quite obvious to Larissa, was a lady of leisure.

"I am so very pleased you've arrived." She led Larissa

by the hand through the double doors. "Come along, now. Come now, don't dawdle."

The drawing room was decorated in blue and white. The blue flower-patterned drapes were tied back on the sides of a bow window. Tall windows on the adjacent wall gave an unobstructed view of the lush garden that lay beyond.

Ivy pulled Larissa onto the blue sofa next to her. "We have so much to talk about. So much to learn about one another."

"My lady—" Larissa began, addressing her new found relative as the butler had.

"No, no, not *my lady* to you. Aunt. No, Aunt Ivy." The aunt pressed one of Larissa's gloved hands to her cheek. "I think that sounds wonderful don't you, dear?"

Aunt Ivy was perhaps a bit odd, but Larissa found her more and more to her liking.

"All right, Aunt Ivy it is." She smiled, feeling a bit shy. "Aunt Ivy, I wish to thank you for your generosity."

"Generosity? My dear girl, I would not—could not have it any other way. The only daughter of my brother. Alfred." Her voice cracked with emotion. She blotted the corner of her eyes with a fine handkerchief which appeared from nowhere. "Poor dear, such a brave soldier. I cannot abandon you. You are my only flesh and blood relative." The handkerchief disappeared, and her mood lightened. "And now, I have simply the best news for you, dear. We are about to embark on a most exciting adventure. I'm nearly all packed and ready to go."

"Go? Go where?" Could any new adventure prove more exciting than her trip here? Larissa found the notion hard to imagine.

"Now that you're out of the schoolroom and all grown up, I have planned to give you a Season."

"A Season? You don't mean we're going to London?"

"Exactly!"

"How? I mean, I thought . . . what about the money?"

"Dear, don't worry about finances. Although I am not rich, I've managed to tuck away a bit, and with some of what your father has left you we've a most comfortable sum. Do remove your bonnet and gloves, my dear. Our tea will arrive momentarily."

Larissa untied the ribbons under her chin and took her time removing her bonnet. She hadn't thought her family had any money to speak of, let alone money for her. Then again, she knew so little about her father. He was a military man. After her mother died, he had her placed in the Miss Simmons' Seminary for Young Ladies. It had been years since she had seen him last. Moreover, she could count all the times she had seen him in her whole life on her fingers.

Moments later, a maid entered and set a tea tray on the low table in front of them. "You see, here is our tea now." Ivy took up the pot and filled their cups. "Now where were we? Oh yes, London.

"I've convinced that dreadful nephew of mine to open his townhouse on Curzon Street for us." She leaned closer to whisper in confidence. "I'm glad none of my blood runs in his veins. A simple ghastly sort, he is. Enough about him." With the wave of her hand she dismissed the subject. "Having no daughters of my own deprived me of sharing such activities as come-outs, and such. But I can spoil you to my heart's content, my dear. Now, about our trip." She gazed wide-eyed at Larissa. "I can't tell you how terribly excited I am. I simply cannot wait to leave."

"But I have only just arrived," Larissa interrupted while Aunt Ivy drained her cup.

"Of course, we'll wait for a few days. Give you time to rest up. Katherine, she's my maid, is still busy packing."

"You've three trunks standing already."

"I know, dear. Katherine will see to it I do not forget anything. She has been with me forever. I'm sure I couldn't manage without her. She is very talented with a needle, and can make the plainest frock a modiste's delight." Ivy took up the pot and refilled her cup. She regarded Larissa's drab brown serge with an alarmingly critical eye. "We will need new gowns and dresses made for you, my dear. An entirely new wardrobe might suit you, along with the new ball gowns we shall require for your come-out. We shall take care of everything as soon as we are settled in London. Do tell me, do you know how to dance?"

"Well," Larissa set her cup on the saucer and held them firm upon her lap, "we did learn the Scottish Reel and Country dances at the seminary."

"The Quadrille?"

"No."

"The Waltz?"

"No!" Larissa gasped and placed her hand at her throat. "I have heard it is the most scandalous of dances. Miss Simmons would never allow such depravity to corrupt her students."

"I'm sure you will have your chance to dance it." Aunt Ivy's eyes sparkled with excitement and she gave a girlish giggle. "Do you speak any foreign languages?"

"French and Latin."

"Latin? That's useless. Only dead Romans speak Latin."

Larissa momentarily considered the idea of dead Romans speaking Latin until her aunt interrupted.

"Do you sew or embroider?" her aunt continued.

"Yes, I am accomplished in both. Miss Simmons required every student to be capable of repairing and sewing her own clothes."

"Well, we need not go that far. Just that you know how is quite enough. Your musical abilities?"

"I am accounted to be fair on the pianoforte."

"All right, then. We shall engage a dancing master as soon as we arrive in Town."

Larissa did not feel elated after her dance lesson with Monsieur Dubois. She felt tired. How long had she been in London now? Two weeks? Or was it three?

"I don't think I will ever get used to these city hours," Larissa sighed. If not for her growling stomach to keep her awake, she'd want her bed instead of the dining room. "Sleeping late, eating late, and attending parties until the small hours of the morning? Aunt, are such things actually done?"

"Not only are they done, dear, in the *beau monde* it is the only way to live." Ivy placed her arm around Larissa's shoulder. "One must be fashionable to be in favor." Ivy's eyebrows rose high over her wide eyes. "And one always wishes to be in favor."

"I suppose you know best, Aunt," Larissa confessed. She didn't have the slightest notion what it took to stay *in favor* with Society. Larissa tried to ignore the continual rumbling of her stomach and lifted her book to pass the time until supper.

"Homer?" Ivy cried, catching the name on the spine. "Oh, my dear, you should not be reading that. You do not want to come across as a bluestocking."

"Aunt, one's interest in books and art does not make one a bluestocking. Does it?"

"No. But thinking and having opinions tends to foster such an impression. One must give an unfettered, vacant impression." Ivy displayed her best imitation. "That's what the gentleman of quality want, not a girl with ideas bobbing about her head. No, no, no. That would not do at all."

"No?" Larissa questioned, still not fully understanding the details.

Ivy gave a sigh. "Not that you need concern yourself yet. You should not feel you must marry this year."

"Marry?" Larissa felt a jolt of panic rush through her. "Aunt, I have only just turned eighteen. Marry? The thought never entered my mind."

"Of course, if you find someone you wish to marry . . . then that would be another matter entirely. But there are so many things one should know."

Larissa remained silent, waiting for her aunt to divulge her pearls of wisdom.

"Your words, your tone of voice, how to address your betters. The use of the fan, shoulders, and eyes." Ivy wrung her hands in her lap. "So much to remember. There is so little time." She looked at Larissa who regarded her with undivided interest. "Do not worry. I will not disappoint you. You shall be ready, when the time comes."

"I'm not worried, Aunt."

Ivy took one of Larissa's hands and gave it a gentle squeeze. "Oh, my dear, if you only knew." Her eyes widened. "There are things you must know when in the company of men. What to say, what to do. What *not* to do," her voice squeaked.

"Not to do?"

"Places to avoid."

"Avoid?"

"Oh, yes. Being alone for one thing. You must *never* be alone with a man."

"*Never?* Is it really that bad?"

"Always have a proper chaperone." Ivy's hand flew to her cheek as she contemplated the implications of such an action. "It would ruin your reputation to be caught without one. Men can be such . . ."

"Yes?"

"Such . . . base creatures. Animals." A flush crept up Ivy's neck, spilling onto her cheeks. "The very worst place—the dark walk at Vauxhall Gardens. You mustn't ever let a man lure you there."

"No, of course not," she agreed, not wanting to cause her aunt further distress. Still, Larissa was not exactly clear what horrible thing would happen if she were to do what her aunt had expressly warned against.

Chapter Six

The Earl of Rushton viewed himself in his full-length glass. He shifted from his right to his left with military precision, admiring the results of the diligent labors of his valet, Georges.

All in all, Uncle Cyrus seemed pleased with his new wardrobe. A dark blue fitted coat of superfine, cream knee breeches and cream stockings with black slippers. In the center of his crisp, snow-white cravat, which Randall instructed Georges to starch lightly, sat an ostentatious sapphire, a silent reminder of his wealth.

Randall found the earl resistant to his new hairstyle. Rushton proclaimed the effort to be venturesome, to say the least, and fought Randall at every step of its undertaking.

"Cut locks cannot be replaced," his Uncle Cyrus cautioned, feeling the horror of cropping the lengthy strand he used to feign a full head of hair.

"A wealth of hair cannot be simulated, Uncle," Randall had responded. "You must make the most of what you have. Women will accentuate your positive qualities."

"And what if the gentler sex deems it appropriate to point out my inadequacies?"

Randall gave a thoughtful smile. "Those would be the women to avoid, wouldn't they?"

Rushton's eyes shot open in realization. "Ah, just so! You are right once again."

"Trust me, Uncle," Randall said in total confidence. "As an eligible earl at Almack's, you won't be ignored." After that discussion, the length of hair in question had been removed.

Rushton fingered his cravat and managed to tear himself away from his glass. "Well, let's be off, shall we? Soon the Season will grind to a halt and then where will I be?"

"Uncle, the Season has only just begun."

"I plan to put every moment to good use. My marriage to your Aunt Constance was arranged, but we grew to love one another, and it was that love"—he punctuated the statement with a forefinger, nearly stabbing Randall's face—"that grew over the years. I know now that love is the only reason to marry. I know the *ton* would not find it fashionable, but what do I care!

"Young or old, rich or poor, it shall not matter to me, for I plan to marry for love. If love eludes me, then I shall not marry. I never intended to replace your Aunt Constance, God rest her soul." Rushton crossed himself. "But I believe she would understand my wanting to remarry."

"I'm sure she would, Uncle. I don't think she would want you to remain alone." Randall felt eternally grateful he did not feel the need to join his uncle in the petticoat line.

Almack's. The weekly gathering of the fashionable and titled. He dreaded being here. It had been two years since Randall had set foot inside its auspicious doors. And just as he had expected, not much within those hallowed walls had changed.

There were the same types of young girls and their matchmaking mamas. Different names, different faces, but they would all look and act the same as the last time he attended.

Randall and his uncle proceeded through the room, reacquainting themselves with the elite guests who were lucky enough to be in attendance. Randall noticed Rushton kept his observant eyes focused mainly on the fairer sex in the crowd.

From across the room, Randall recognized Lady Dorothea Brookhurst. She had been a beauty years ago when he had first set eyes on her. How she had blossomed!

Randall had never seen such loveliness and grace combined in one woman. Luckily he was not a stranger to her and he need not wait for an introduction. There was no sign of men inundating her. He did not know why, but decided not to question his good fortune and did not delay making his move.

"Excuse me, Uncle Cyrus. I see someone I need to reacquaint myself with."

"Of course, my boy. Do go ahead." Rushton waved him on.

Randall could feel his lips curve into a gracious smile. He was well pleased indeed. Smoothing a hand over his fine waistcoat, Randall shifted and straightened a crease in the arm of his jacket before advancing across the room.

As he neared Lady Dorothea, he thought her radiant hair surely must consist of the rays of the sun. Her eyes, of celestial blue, glistened. Her lips would cause the reddest of roses to pale. He need not go on to see that she was a delight to behold. The grace of her arms only hinted at the lithe movements of her body. Every turn, sway, and dip bespoke her statuesque elegance.

"Lady Dorothea," he greeted and sketched a bow.

"Why, Sir Randall, is it not?" she remarked, surprised. "It has been an age, has it not?"

"It has been quite some time since we last met." His eyes met her cool stare. "Would it be presumptuous to inquire if you have an opening on your dance card?"

Dorothea ran her finger down the dance card. She inscribed *Sir Randall Trent.*

"The next waltz," she announced to his ultimate delight.

Randall could not believe his luck, a waltz! "I shall return shortly to claim my dance then." In parting, he took her gloved hand in his and raised it to his lips. Moving away from Lady Dorothea, Randall scanned the room for his uncle.

"Is that you, Trent?" Sir Thomas White made his approach, followed by Donald Sinclair.

"Sir Thomas," Randall greeted. "Is that Sinclair with you?"

"What the devil are you doing here?" The surprise on

Thomas' face was only surpassed by the amazement on Donald Sinclair's.

"Wouldn't have thought you'd step into this place unless your life depended on it," Sinclair added.

"Or unless you think it's time for a wife." Randall knew Thomas must have thought that even further from the truth.

"You've nearly got the whole of it. It's my uncle who is here to find a new countess."

"Ah, Rushton," Thomas recalled, pointing him out on the dance floor.

Sinclair peered around to look. "Who is that exquisite lady with your uncle?"

Randall craned to catch a glimpse of Rushton's dance partner. All he could see was the smile on his Uncle Cyrus' face. Dressed all in white, his dance partner was lovely with her golden hair swept atop her head. Not the almost white-gold of Lady Dorothea's hair, but guinea gold.

"Rather. She is a pure confection," Thomas gasped.

Donald Sinclair gave a sigh and grasped his chest near the area of his heart. "I believe I am in love."

"Sinclair, you're in love with anything wearing a white frock," Thomas accused.

The country dance brought Rushton into closer range. So close that Randall could see the fair face of his uncle's dance partner. It was then Randall felt all cheerful expression fade.

It couldn't be. It couldn't possibly be.

Miss Larissa Quinn?

Chapter Seven

What happened to rusticating in the wilds of West-moreland?

A lie. Clearly another lie she'd told. And why not? Randall had lost count of how many falsehoods Larissa Quinn had told during the short amount of time they had shared. Now she was dancing with his Uncle Cyrus.

What stories would she be telling him? Was she now passing herself off as an heiress? Or perhaps a princess from some faroff land?

"Sir Randall? Sir Randall?" Sinclair repeated. "Do you know who that creature of sheer loveliness is?"

"Ah—I know *of* her." Randall wanted the acquaintance between Larissa and his uncle to be nipped in the bud. He would not stand for his uncle to continue with *her*. Uncle Cyrus had to be warned, and warned right away. "You must excuse me, gentlemen." In set determination, Randall started across the room to deliver the unpleasant news.

"Wait a bit, Trent." Sinclair took hold of Randall's sleeve. "You're not leaving without me."

Randall pulled his arm free. "You are more than welcome to her, my friend." Randall noticed how Sinclair's face brightened. Did Sinclair consider him a threat? Randall's solitary interest in the chit was keeping her away from his uncle. Sinclair could have Miss Quinn all to himself.

As far as Randall was concerned, it was Larissa who should take care. Describing Donald Sinclair as a rake might be going too far; he merely enjoyed the ladies. However, Randall noticed Sir Thomas White was the first to approach Larissa. Sinclair's unnecessary concern about Randall's intentions had caused him to be fourth in line.

Randall found his Uncle Cyrus and ushered him away from where Larissa held court.

"I find her most agreeable," Rushton muttered. He glanced several times over his shoulder to glimpse Larissa.

"Agreeable?" Randall took hold of Rushton's shoulders and squared his uncle in front of him. "Listen to me, Uncle, she's *persona non grata.*" Randall saw the faraway expression in Rushton's face and interpreted it as a potentially ominous omen. "Someone to stay away from. Very far away from." Randall could see by the vacant look on his uncle's face he still wasn't making any progress.

"Know her, do you?" Rushton remarked in a knowing way.

"Let me just say if I had known she was on the ship up the Severn, rather than keep her company, I'd plunge into the drink and take my chances with a pack of circling sharks." Randall checked his uncle's expression. "You do take my meaning, don't you, Uncle?"

Still looking in Larissa's direction, Rushton held a steady, affable smile on his face. "I heard what you said, dear boy."

"Not what I said, my meaning. She's not one to be trifled with, I tell you."

Rushton stared toward the heavens and continued in a moist, emotion-filled tone. "Your Aunt Constance used to go on about that—meaning, morals, life's lessons and such, God rest her soul."

"Uncle Cyrus!" Randall was now all but shouting.

"What is it?"

"Miss Larissa Quinn," he reminded.

"Ah, yes!" Rushton glanced across the room at Larissa for a reminder. "I find her quite agreeable indeed. Very charming."

"No, not her, my warning about her. You do understand the point I'm getting at, don't you?"

"Yes, oh yes. I got the point, dear boy. Just as well, I'm probably too old for her anyway." Rushton went on thoughtfully. "I defer to your judgment. I entirely agree she is more suited for a much younger man."

Thank goodness, Randall thought in relief, his Uncle Cyrus had given up any thoughts about furthering his relation with Miss Larissa Quinn.

"Excuse me. Miss Quinn?" It was a scant hour later when Randall made his respectful approach. His actions mimicked the many suitors who came before him.

Clearly shocked by his presence, Larissa stammered, "S-sir Randall, is it not?"

"Yes, that's right." He smiled. "You remembered."

"It is unlikely I should ever forget." Her words were innocuous, but the tone spoke volumes.

"Would it be possible to speak to you alone for a moment?"

"Alone?" Larissa glanced around. For whom, Randall was not sure. "Is it allowed?"

"We shall be on the terrace, in plain sight of the entire room."

"I am promised for the next set," she said, catching her lower lip with her teeth.

"I assure you, we shall not be long." Randall held his arm out and waited.

Larissa placed her hand lightly atop his arm and allowed him to escort her into the night air.

Once away from the other guests, Randall spun to face her. "What the devil do you think you are doing here?"

"I see no reason you should speak to me in that tone. I have not done anything wrong."

"Haven't done anything wrong?" Randall glanced into the ballroom making sure they had not drawn unnecessary attention. "Do you know what would happen should word get out about . . . about . . ." His voice softened to a whisper, "The incident at The Blue Boar Inn?"

"If you do not wish anyone to know about *the incident,* then I suggest you do not speak of it. Even as a point of reference."

"I want to forget it ever happened. I don't even want to acknowledge I know you."

"Well, it's a bit late for that, is it not? By addressing me by name, you've just told an entire roomful of London Society that we are acquainted. Not only know me, but know me well. As I have just agreed to see you . . . alone. And at your request, I might add."

Randall stood silent. She was right. It had been a foolish maneuver on his part.

"By kissing me, you've made yourself quite well-known to me. I could hardly ignore you, could I?" Larissa's gaze was hard.

"I think not. Well, you can take satisfaction in knowing it will never happen again."

"No?" she squeaked. Almost as if she were disappointed.

"No," he repeated, his voice firm.

"Was it so very improper?" Her eyes held him riveted. Randall knew he could not allow himself to be swayed by her innocent appearance. He, more than anyone, should know better.

She'd told him that she had grown up in the confines of a girls' seminary. He wondered if it was true. Surely, they must have taught more than reading and writing, something about the social graces. After all, she had known how to dance.

"No, it is not proper for a man to kiss a woman in public—even if they happen to be married to each other. It's blatant, outrageous behavior. Wholly unsuitable. That woman sitting across from us, Mrs. Briggs, drove me into doing something rash." He swallowed hard. Watching her for a moment longer, he inhaled her scent, fresh and fragrant. He remembered the sweet taste of her full lips.

Now they were quite alone in the garden and at that moment he found her very desirable.

"Oh" was Larissa's only comment. How could she tell him she had enjoyed it? He had been on her thoughts since they had parted. A single day had not passed when she did not think of him. "It is permitted to partake in such activities when alone, then?" She stared up at him, looking for guidance.

Sir Randall tugged at the inside of his cravat with a finger. "I shouldn't even be speaking to you of such things."

"How shall I ever understand if I am not told?" she replied with a hint of frustration.

"What I mean to say is, I should not be the one informing you of subjects of such a personal and delicate nature," Sir Randall said in his own defense. "I hope you enjoy your Season, for I do not expect we shall meet again." With those parting words, he sketched a bow and left.

Larissa watched Sir Randall reenter the room and disappear into the crowd. Sir Randall Trent was the last person she had expected to see. He had been traveling to see his uncle, if she was not mistaken, and London had never been mentioned as far as she could recall.

Still, he was here. Sharing the same city, sharing the same ballroom, and sharing the same memory. Only he wanted nothing more to do with her. If he would not be willing to indulge her, she would find someone who would.

Larissa strolled into the room, tapping the end of her folded fan on her fingertips. He wasn't the only man around. She surveyed the room, there were dozens. She liked what she had felt with Sir Randall when he kissed her and decided she'd have more.

Indeed, there would be no stopping her.

Randall kept company with his uncle between the next several sets. As anticipated, there was no lack of interest in Rushton. What did surprise him was his uncle's stamina, participating in every dance. Randall eagerly anticipated the approaching waltz, the waltz he planned to share with Lady Dorothea.

His attention drifted from the languorous Lady Dorothea, whom he suspected might be striking an attitude for his benefit, and returned to Larissa. Observing the surrounding throng, Randall saw she did not lack attention, for her popularity appeared to grow with every passing minute.

Randall had broached the dance floor and now stood at Lady Dorothea's side. No more thoughts of Larissa, he told himself, for Lady Dorothea was more to his taste. Refined, subdued, and above all, suitable.

With a smile, he tucked her kid-gloved hand into the crook of his arm and led her to the dance floor. During their dance, while he held her close in his arms, guiding her around the floor, he further contemplated his partner. He thought that surely, by now, Lady Dorothea would have married. Sir Randall added to her list of engaging qualities, charm, delightful company, and accomplished dancing.

Knowing he would be expected to call on the morrow, the last thing he wanted to do was send a footman with his card. That was not the message he wanted to relay. Randall was interested, he repeatedly told himself, deeply interested in Lady Dorothea.

He took his commitment to his Uncle Cyrus seriously and could not abandon him while he took the time to pay a call on his latest love interest. After all, Randall was not the one in London to find a wife.

Strangely enough, he did not find the idea of marriage disturbing in the least, and if Lady Dorothea filled that position, so much the better. She was a girl who knew her place, knew how to act properly. He would ultimately be better off with her.

It was too early to tell whether Lady Dorothea adequately filled his requirements for a wife and he looked forward to exploring that avenue. If he had the time, that is. At the present, he did not. He had to attend to Uncle Cyrus.

Randall felt he should mention his inability to pay her proper attention, and that he would rectify the situation once matters with his uncle sorted themselves out.

"Lady Dorothea, I would love to take you on a drive tomorrow." Randall glanced across the room to his uncle.

"Then, pray tell, why don't you?" Dorothea directed her eyes to Randall. They were breathtaking, wide, celestial blue eyes framed by long, lovely lashes.

"To tell the truth, I am not here to indulge myself. I am to accompany my uncle."

"Your uncle? And who is your uncle?"

"The Earl of Rushton."

"I see," Dorothea replied.

"He is depending on me. I cannot shirk my responsibility to him." It didn't seem to make a difference to her that he had an earl for an uncle. Gads, half the room must have earls for uncles, if not dukes.

"I understand. Nor would I even ask it of you." She gave a wistful sigh and a longing look. "How dutiful you are, Sir Randall. It is such an honorable quality."

"Tomorrow, I shall do my utmost to pay a call."

"Oh, please do." Lady Dorothea stared at Randall with her wide eyes. "But, I would understand completely if you cannot find the time to do so. One cannot fault a dutiful gentleman."

"I am sure this is not the last we shall meet."

"I am sure you are correct." The corners of her rosebud lips curved up. She bestowed upon Randall the most perfect smile he had ever seen, charming him to the tips of his dancing slippers.

Chapter Eight

The following day, Randall accompanied Uncle Cyrus on his morning calls, thus preventing him from making his own call on Lady Dorothea. Sending a card did not properly convey his feelings, so he did the next best thing—sent a flower bouquet with a personal note.

The lightness in Randall's step abated once he and his uncle stepped into the Curzon Street townhouse, residence of Miss Larissa Quinn and her aunt. To Randall's great relief, they found the occupants not at home. Before leaving, Rushton left his calling card with the butler.

Once inside the carriage, Randall could not prevent the image of Larissa from flickering into his mind, and it did so with astounding ease. She *had* looked lovely last night, her golden hair pulled atop her head, curled tendrils framing her face, teasing him to brush them back. The excited look in her eyes was the look of an innocent who was experiencing the wonder of her first lavish social affair. He had not seen an expression like that in years.

Randall admitted he felt an attraction to her, but in the next lucid thought, he quickly dismissed the idea of keeping her acquaintance. However, he did wonder what it would have been like to hold her in his arms and dance.

"I'm afraid you've been right all along, my dear boy," Rushton said, breaking the silence.

"Right? About what, Uncle?"

"Miss Quinn, much too young." Rushton shrugged. "Whatever would I do with such loveliness?"

Randall had a few ideas and thought it best to keep them to himself. Although he considered her troublesome, Larissa conjured up feelings in him, feelings best left hidden. He wanted to avoid all thought of her and concentrated on Lady Dorothea to make him forget Larissa. He *hoped* Dorothea would make him forget Larissa.

Just one week later, Randall had the pleasure of sleeping late. It was now scarcely after one in the afternoon. He hadn't risen much later than that in this last week of nonstop parties and balls. He and his uncle had seen the dawn of each new day arrive. Most days since their arrival, Rushton had insisted his nephew accompany him on his round of morning calls that more likely than not seemed to stretch into the late afternoon. Today he was fortunate enough to breakfast at his leisure.

He sat at the table enjoying his coffee and skimming the headlines of the morning paper when his Uncle Cyrus bounded in. "I've found her! I've found her!" Rushton exclaimed. He fairly pranced on the tips of his toes around the length of the long breakfast table with delight. "She is the one! She is the light of my life! The very breath in my body!"

"Already?" Randall folded the paper and set it aside. "Albeit you've been searching day and night. Must have danced with every lady in town by now."

"Haven't you heard a word I've been saying? I said I have found her, my boy!"

"I share your happiness, Uncle. Who is she, pray tell?"

"The Dowager Viscountess Claiborne," his love struck uncle crooned.

The sparkle in Rushton's eyes alluded to the amatory pounding of his heart. Smitten. He was more than smitten, Randall decided. Quite taken, indeed.

"I am to see her tomorrow night at the ball after the opera." Rushton took hold of his nephew's shoulders. "I need to ask a great favor of you, my boy."

Wary by instinct, Randall proceeded with reluctance. "What is it you wish me to do?"

"My angel will only spend time with me if I can assure her ward has a suitable escort." Rushton looked hopefully at his nephew.

"Oh, no." Randall feared what might come next.

"It is only for the ball that follows the opera. It is such a short while." Rushton stared directly into Randall's eyes. "I've already promised."

"Tell me you didn't," Randall said, knowing full well his uncle already had. Worse than having to attend the Season was being forced to tolerate some maid on her third season.

"I knew I could count on you, my boy," Rushton crowed

with delight. "I'm off to bed," he announced. "I'm going to need my beauty sleep. Haven't had much lately." He gave a burst of laughter and rocked his head. "If I *can* fall asleep that is." With that, he gave a knowing wink and spun with delight out of the room.

Randall smiled, amused at the sight of his uncle. Then all of a sudden he realized, now that Rushton had found his next countess, his time constraints would ease. Uncle Cyrus' good fortune was Randall's good fortune as well. He could use the phaeton to take Lady Dorothea for a drive in Hyde Park that very afternoon. He wasted no time in dispatching a note to her.

"I say, Miss Larissa, is that not a new bonnet?" She and Lord Fenton Harding had arrived just at the height of the fashionable hour at Hyde Park. Lord Fenton gave the horses their heads to walk along the busy, well-traveled path.

Larissa peeked out at him from beneath the brim. "Why yes, it is new. Do you like it?" She found it tedious that Lord Fenton touched only upon the most correct subjects for a lady's discussion. Ladies' fashions, last night's social gatherings and the latest *on dit*.

"It's quite fetching," he complimented in his proper manner. Perhaps it was too proper.

"Thank you," she replied. What Larissa found fetching was Lord Fenton's smile.

"Miss Larissa, did you happen to take notice of Miss Uppington-Styles last evening?"

"Miss Uppington-Styles?" Larissa tilted her head in quizzical contemplation, holding the loose ribbons from her bonnet. She caught Lord Fenton's fine profile as he awaited his answer.

His aristocratic nose, while slender, was not sharp. His chin fell to a nice point from a strong, wide jaw. She regarded how his slender yet strong hands handled the reins with a gentle firmness. She could just as easily imagine the way in which his long, tapered fingers would hold her fast and deliver a gentle touch or a warm caress.

How much longer did she have to wait? She wanted him to take her hand into his and press it. She wanted him to pull her into his arms and kiss her breathless, just as Sir Randall had.

"Miss Larissa?"

Larissa found herself gazing into Lord Fenton's face. "I am sorry, my lord. We were speaking of Miss Uppington-Styles, were we not?"

"Yes, that's right." He gave a jovial social laugh. "She wore a simply dazzling raspberry-colored gown."

"Raspberry? Are you sure?"

"I believe so. Too purple to be scarlet, and too red to be violet. I thought raspberry a most apt description."

"What a brilliant observation," Larissa gushed, doing her best London Miss imitation.

Lord Fenton continued to speak while he and Larissa acknowledged other fashionable guests in passing carriages. Larissa spied a somewhat familiar gig, not too far off in the distance. It took a gentle curve, approaching from the opposite direction, coming toward them. The dark green phaeton with a fine yellow stripe finally drew close enough for her to see the passengers.

Sir Randall Trent recognized Larissa Quinn at once and

drew back on the ribbons, pulling his team to a sliding and disruptive halt. The horses neighed, shaking their heads in protest. After they settled and stood quiet an awkward moment of silence ensued.

"I would not wish to speak out of place," Larissa began, her voice, not much more than a whisper, was meant for her escort and not for Randall. "However, I do believe someone must say something."

It was only after Larissa spoke that Randall realized both transports stood facing one another at a standstill, caught in an uncomfortable social circumstance.

"I'm afraid I do not know the proper order of introducing a younger son of a duke to a baronet." Larissa's attention darted from Fenton to Randall.

"Nearly any titled person ranks above a baronet," came the soft reminder next to her.

Larissa gave an awkward smile. "Then, Lord Fenton, may I present Sir Randall Trent. Sir Randall, Lord Fenton Harding."

The men tipped their hats and exchanged gracious social pleasantries. All of it properly done. All of it polite and yet very staged.

Randall observed the awkward silence that followed. Larissa and Lord Fenton stared at him. He realized he had not performed the same introductions for Lady Dorothea.

"Would you be so kind, Sir Randall, as to introduce your guest?" Lord Fenton drawled.

Randall's head snapped toward Lady Dorothea who remained quiet. "Why, yes of course," he faltered. "Lady Dorothea Brookhurst, may I present Lord Fenton Hartley."

Lord Fenton gave a chuckle. "No, no, you've quite mistaken, Sir Randall. It's *Harding*."

Randall feigned an amused chuckle of his own, joining Lord Fenton. "Yes, of course. Lord Fenton . . . *Harding* and Miss Larissa Quinn. I did get *that* right, didn't I?"

"Spot on," Lord Fenton exclaimed with enthusiasm.

Lady Dorothea enunciated a polite "How do you do" to each and said nothing more.

"Well, hate to run," Lord Fenton interjected, "but I fear we must. Good day to you."

"You as well," Randall bid, taking up his ribbons. "Enjoy the remainder of your drive."

Randall signaled his horses to move. He rested his elbows on his knees and pondered. Why on earth couldn't Larissa at least have taken an interest in a man? A real man. Harding wasn't a man, he was a confounded piece of fluff. Randall did not care. He need not concern himself with her any longer. Larissa was out of his life for good.

Randall felt the touch on his leg. It was the pink gloved hand of Lady Dorothea. Gads, he had nearly forgotten her again. Bumping into Larissa had distracted him. What a cad he was.

He looked down the tunnel of Lady Dorothea's poke bonnet. Large blue eyes framed by full lashes gazed back at him, drawing every bit of his attention, rendering him speechless.

"Are you quite all right, Sir Randall?"

Randall sighed. She was all he needed in a wife—considerate and beautiful, and she had an uncanny ability to make him forget all about Larissa.

Chapter Nine

"**I** beg your pardon, Sir Randall," Laurie interrupted.

Randall looked up from his book. "Yes, Laurie, what is it?"

The butler had a regal air about him. "His lordship wishes me to remind you of the opera performance you will be attending this evening."

"I'd be hard pressed to forget it." Randall cracked a smile. "Uncle Cyrus has been talking of nothing but the opera."

"I hadn't realized my lord was overly fond of the theater, sir."

Randall rested the book on his chest. "I believe it is a lady who has caught his interest."

Laurie's left eyebrow lifted, while keeping his austere facial expression intact.

"Well, I think enough said, really." Randall glanced at the page to find where he had left off. "Thank you."

"Yes, sir."

Still seated, Randall noted Laurie had not left. "Is there something else?"

"I believe it was the earl's intention, sir, to have you ready yourself for this evening's festivities," Laurie continued in a disapproving tone.

"You can't be serious." Randall once again lowered the book.

Laurie said nothing, but his expression told Randall he had meant every word.

"It's much too early," Randall commented. "I've only just had tea."

"That was more than two hours ago, sir," Laurie corrected.

"Was it?" Randall regarded the butler in quizzical contemplation.

"I believe so, sir."

"Well, Laurie, regardless of when I took tea, I contend it is not time to ready myself for the opera. I shan't bow to his lordship's whim this time. Is that understood?"

"As you say, sir," the butler replied in elevated tones.

"I do say. Now off with you," Randall stated with unquestionable firmness. He waved his book, dismissing the messenger.

Not two minutes later, Rushton strode into the library. "Odd's fish!" he exclaimed, not at all pleased to see Randall still in his day clothes. "Why haven't you dressed? Didn't Laurie tell you we'd soon be off?" Randall opened his mouth to answer. His uncle didn't give him a chance to speak. "It's not like him to take what I say into disregard."

"He did tell me, Uncle," Randall finally managed to get it in. "I just didn't think he was serious."

"Of course I am serious."

Apparently he *was* serious. The earl was dressed to the nines.

"Come along, boy, come along, you need to change. We'll be late for sure." Rushton took the book out of Randall's hand, pulled him to his feet, and gave him a sturdy push toward the door.

"Late?" Randall consulted his watch. "Why, Uncle, we have hours until we need leave."

"Hours?" Rushton gawked at his nephew as if he had sprouted a second head. He dropped the book onto the small table. "No, no. We need to be there when the curtain goes up."

"You want to *see* the opera?"

"I plan on seeing the entire performance, from start to finish."

"What?" Randall was now clearly confused. "Which opera is it?"

"It's . . ." Rushton stopped. "It doesn't matter. You'll be sleeping straight through it regardless."

"You're right," he agreed without contest and set out for his room to change.

The Earl of Rushton led the way to his theater box and sat in the front. Upon entering, Randall eased into a chair behind his uncle. A quick glance at the other boxes told him they were the only occupants on their level. Within minutes, the overture started, the curtain rose and Randall could not prevent his eyelids from lowering.

"Wake up, lad." Rushton seized Randall by the arm,

waking him after what felt like only moments of sleep. "Come on, now," his uncle urged, impatient.

"Is it time to leave?" Randall mumbled, rising to his feet still half asleep.

"Don't be an ass. We're going to see my beloved angel."

"Oh, only intermission." Randall stood, gave a sigh and smoothed his recently assaulted sleeve. Trudging behind his uncle, he wondered about this paragon of womanhood his uncle had gone on about for the last two days. On the other hand, he was quite willing to put off the inevitable meeting of the dowdy ward.

Randall came to a sudden stop behind Rushton, who gave no advance notice of his abrupt halt. The earl pointed at the heavy brocade drape. "She's in here. In here, my boy," he said anxiously, taking a moment to primp. "Do I look all right?"

"You look fine, Uncle." Randall gave him a brush to the back of his coat and removed a mote of lint. Rushton parted the curtains and stepped into the box with his nephew close behind.

Once he stepped inside, Randall stood stock-still. "It's her," he gasped, shocked, no—stunned by the woman inside.

"Of course it's her." Rushton's face reflected his delight at the nearness of his *amour*.

Randall clamped onto his uncle's arm, preventing him from advancing. "Why didn't you tell me?"

"Why ever do you think we came all the way over here, nodcock? She is the Dowager Viscountess—"

"No, no, Uncle, the *her* I am referring to is Miss Quinn." Randall's eyes widened.

"Didn't think I needed to. I thought you made your feelings about her quite clear the other night," Rushton recalled. "Wanted her for yourself, if I'm not mistaken."

"Mistaken?" How could his uncle have come up with that misapprehension? "You couldn't be further from the truth."

"Well, my boy, there are truths and there are truths, aren't there?" Rushton pried himself from Randall's grip. "Ah, well then, we'll have to make the best of the situation, won't we?" The earl advanced toward the dowager viscountess.

"The best?" Randall echoed to himself. "I can hardly stand to be in the same room with her, let alone in the same theater box."

With the viscountess' dainty gloved hand in his, Rushton pointed in Randall's direction. "Viscountess Claiborne, may I present my nephew, Sir Randall Trent."

"How do you do?" the very handsome, matronly woman replied. The plumes on her turban swayed with every movement of her head.

Randall accepted her proffered hand and kissed the air some two inches above. "I have heard so much about you, my lady." He straightened enough to meet her eyes. "All favorable, I assure you," he added with a savory smile.

"I see charm runs in your family, Rushton," she murmured to the earl and pulled her hand free. The dowager extended her arm, indicating Larissa next to her. "Sir Randall, may I present my niece, Miss Larissa Quinn."

Randall gave an easy smile. "Charmed, Miss Quinn."

"How nice to see you, Sir Randall." She dropped into the shallowest of curtsies.

However, it was evident to Randall she had not meant her kind words.

"I thought I would not again have the pleasure."

A fleeting look at his uncle and the dowager told Randall they were in a world of their own. Randall drew Larissa aside, allowing the couple their privacy. "No need to flatter yourself. I am here strictly on my uncle's behalf."

"And I only tolerate you because of my aunt's happiness."

"You never told me your aunt is a viscountess."

"You never told me your uncle is an earl." Larissa glanced at her blissful aunt and turned back to Randall. "There is no need to treat me like some unwelcome distant relative."

"If my uncle has his way that is exactly what you will become."

Randall eyed his uncle, lost to the current of love that was pulling him farther and farther into its persuasive grasp. The viscountess, it seemed, was equally lost.

"He means to marry her." Randall sighed.

A whimsical smile brightened Larissa's face. "Does he?"

"And to that end, I have promised to escort you to the ball following the opera."

"You need not concern yourself in that quarter. I have a qualified companion."

No doubt she referred to that overpuffed pigeon, Fenton. "Who chooses to, or not to, pay you court is none of my concern."

"You speak those words with such ease. However," she smiled, "the green pallor of your face is clashing horribly with the blue of your jacket."

"Me? Jealous? Don't flatter yourself."

"It is you who flatters *yourself*." Larissa sat in her chair, demonstrating, she was at ease. "You must think highly of yourself if you think I'm concerned whether you care for me." She folded her arms in front of her and turned away from him, presenting her profile.

"No higher than you think of yourself, I'm certain." Randall crossed his arms and pivoted in the opposite direction, displaying his profile in hostility.

He need not accept this type of behavior from her. Randall was doing her a favor by assuming the responsibility of an escort. He could be just as obstinate as she. Out of the corner of his eye he noticed she did not move one iota. Therefore, he held his pose. He schooled his features into placid granite, refusing to soften.

"Oh look, Rushton," the viscountess pointed at Larissa and Randall. "The children are playing. Persephone and Hades at odds, are they not?"

Rushton shrugged and followed her as she moved to the posing pair for a closer study.

Hades, indeed, Randall mused. "We should be going, Uncle." Randall broke form. "The second act should be starting any moment."

Rushton took the dowager's hand in his and brought it to his lips. "*Adieu,* my lady, until we meet at the ball."

"Of course, my lord," she replied. To Randall she seemed somewhat distracted. "I have it!" The viscountess whirled to face the exiting guests. "Deucalion and Pyrrha, surveying Parnassus."

Randall eased back into his chair. Uncle Cyrus took a seat in the front row of the box. Struggling to fend off the hold of Morpheus, Randall glanced around. Most of the upper boxes still stood empty, and would remain so until nearly the end of the evening.

He observed Viscountess Claiborne in her box. On stage was the poignant scene where the hero, of whom the heroine's father disapproved, expressed his love. Opera glasses poised in front of the dowager's eyes. She leaned forward to catch every note, to see every expression, to feel every emotion from the performers. Tears spilled onto her cheeks as the hero professed his forbidden love to the heroine.

Randall noted his uncle's attention was directed not toward the stage, but off to the left. Raising his own glass, Randall took a second, closer look to the left—the dowager viscountess. Just to her right, struggling to sit upright was Larissa.

The dim theater light glinted off her golden hair. Her bright eyes glimmered in the dark. She covered her yawn with the back of her right hand. The opera obviously held the same interest for her as it did for him.

After a random search of the lower level, Larissa's wandering gaze drifted to the upper tier. She stopped when she met Randall's conspicuous stare. Randall lowered his glasses. What Larissa's first theater experience lacked in musical entertainment, it compensated for in personal pleasure.

Larissa did not look away. Her inquiring eyes were hidden in the semidarkness. Had Randall nodded off, she could have easily studied him without him noticing as she had during the first half of the evening.

His eyes were blacker than the night. His hair was almost blue in the darkness. The lines of his face, sculpted by the shadows, that face she knew so well was as handsome as she remembered.

Why did he need to behave so rudely toward her? Was it because of their first meeting? Perhaps if they had a proper introduction, things between them would be different. There was no use in wishing for something she could not have. But if he had not cared for her, why did he stare at her so?

Chapter Ten

After the final curtain, Randall and his uncle left their box for the ball. The one thing Randall would definitely not do was disappoint his uncle. Although he dreaded the upcoming event as much as he imagined his uncle looked forward to it.

When they arrived, Rushton charged to the dowager's side. It was all too clear to Randall that the rest of the room vanished from their sight. If his uncle wanted the dowager viscountess as his new countess, Randall would do his utmost to make it come about. He would be the model escort for Larissa, regardless of his personal opinion of her.

Randall turned to address Larissa. He knew she no more cared to dance with him than he with her. However, tonight, he would be more than happy to partner her—for his uncle's sake.

Without a word, Larissa accepted. He led her onto the

dance floor. There she smiled. Trying to present a positive image to the viscountess, Randall thought. At least they could agree on that one item. Or so he hoped.

At the end of the set, Randall took Larissa on his arm toward her aunt, giving a pleasant smile of his own. "I don't want you ruining their happiness," he voiced in threatening tones.

"Me? If anyone is a killjoy it is you."

"Miss Quinn, if we were not in public, I certainly would take delight in . . ."

"What? In what?" Her eyes blazed in fury, never losing her cadence in step beside him.

"Take great joy in bending you over my knee and disciplining you like the spoiled brat you are." He held his false smile in place.

"Spoiled brat?" she gasped and spit back. "You indulgent prig."

"Undisciplined wench."

"Arrogant wastrel."

"Cheeky chit."

"Pretentious fop." Another step brought them in the company of Rushton and Viscountess Claiborne.

"I can see you two are getting along splendidly," the dowager greeted.

"Oh, yes. Famously," Larissa agreed, her glacial eyes upon Randall.

"Quite famously," Randall seconded.

"Did I not tell you, my sweet?" Rushton reassured his *amour*, soothing any doubts she may have harbored.

"I am so very glad you were right, as always." She patted Rushton's hand and disengaged her arm from his. "If you gentlemen will excuse us. I wish to speak to my niece alone for a moment." She turned Larissa to one side and took a few steps away.

"Would you mind if I were to leave you in Sir Randall's care for a dance or two?" the viscountess said to Larissa. "Rushton is a most persuasive man. He assures me you are quite safe with his nephew. I must say, I am quite taken with him myself. I am persuaded he will serve well as an escort."

"No, Aunt. You go right ahead. I'll be fine." Larissa returned to Randall's side. She laced her arm through his and gave him a superb smile, pretending to flourish in his company. Without a doubt, it was solely for her aunt's benefit.

Now that Larissa would be watched over, the dowager viscountess left on Rushton's arm. She leaned toward him and whispered something confidential and they both broke into a hearty bout of laughter, making quite a spectacle of themselves.

"You'd best mind your temper," Larissa warned, watching her aunt retreat.

"You'd best mind your tongue," Randall countered.

"I feel we would both be better off if you left me in Lord Fenton's care when he arrives," Larissa suggested. "And that will leave you to Lady Dorothea."

Randall knew better than anyone how stubborn Larissa was once she got an idea in her head, and his first impulse was to accede. However, he was not one to give in so readily. After all, he had just promised to keep watch over her. He couldn't very well just leave her to someone he hardly knew. Or could he? Randall was tempted, and it might not take much to sway him to her perspective.

"I do not see why we need suffer because of their budding romance," she continued, trying to drive her point across.

"Their 'budding romance' as you put it, is all that I am interested in, at the moment."

"Is it really?" She smiled, her eyes positively glowed. "Wouldn't Lady Dorothea be interested to hear that."

"You leave Lady Dorothea out of this," Randall warned. It would do his case no good for Dorothea to hear of his interest from Larissa.

Larissa tilted her head, looking over his shoulder and gesturing to someone with her fan. "Here she comes now."

Randall turned to see Lady Dorothea approaching at this inopportune moment. "My lady," he greeted, sketching a bow. He couldn't very well put her off now.

"Sir Randall," Dorothea acknowledged. "Miss Quinn."

"Sir Randall was just speaking of you, Lady Dorothea."

"Were you?"

"He was just pondering of your whereabouts, and now"—she shrugged—"here you are. I shall leave you two alone as soon as Lord Fenton makes his appearance." She perused the room and glanced every now and again at the doorway. "I do hope he arrives soon. I find a threesome so awkward, don't you?" Her face brightened. "Ah, here he is now. Lord Fen-ton," Larissa called to him in soprano tones.

"Miss Larissa." Lord Fenton placed a kiss on the back of Larissa's hand, holding it far longer than he needed to. "Lady Dorothea, and Sir Randall, how nice that we meet again."

"How nice," Randall echoed without enthusiasm, playing along with conventional ballroom etiquette.

Larissa interrupted. "Oh, Lord Fenton, I'm afraid I cannot bear to step foot onto the dance floor if I do not find something to drink this instant."

Lord Fenton took this as a personal challenge. "I cannot have you experience another parched moment. Let us find the refreshments." He nodded to Randall and Lady Dorothea. "If you will kindly excuse us."

Randall watched Lord Fenton lead Larissa away. *That presumptuous puppy and that ill-tempered chit most certainly deserve one another*, Randall thought.

"Do you disapprove, Sir Randall?" Dorothea asked.

"Disapprove? Why should I disapprove? I don't give a fig one way or the other." Randall forced himself to look at Lady Dorothea and smiled, taking interest in her. "Your delightful presence is the only thing making this evening worthwhile."

"How kind of you to say," Lady Dorothea remarked. She blushed and in a quick, light flutter waved her fan in front of her face, drawing it downward to stop at the low neckline of her gown. Randall's eyes followed the fan and lingered at her revealing décolletage.

Two evenings later, Aunt Ivy and Larissa readied themselves for an outing to Vauxhall Gardens. Of course, they would never have ventured there without male escort. Aunt Ivy considered the place "an alfresco adventure."

"You look charming, my dear," Ivy praised with maternal pride. "Is it Sir Randall who has put that delicate bloom on you cheek?"

"Oh, Aunt," Larissa sighed, wondering if she should tell her aunt the truth. "I do not care for Sir Randall. In fact I can honestly say we do not rub along well together at all."

"That is very strange, indeed." Ivy placed her hand on her cheek and gave Larissa a puzzled look. "I was under the distinct impression you two got along tolerably."

"Do not mistake my intentions, Aunt. All we *can* do is tolerate each other."

"Oh, I see," Aunt Ivy contemplated. "Well then, if you and Sir Randall are not amiable, there is no reason to torture you with his company. I shall send a note to Rushton, to cancel."

"Oh no, Aunt, you cannot. The earl will be broken-hearted. He is so very taken with you. I do not think he could bear to be without your company for an entire evening." Larissa saw the glint in her aunt's eyes at the mention of Rushton. "And I cannot say you would be pleased, either."

Aunt Ivy gave a surrendering smile.

"Aunt, you have been everything kind to me. I cannot ask you to forsake your own happiness because of my discomfort."

"But what about you, my dear?" Ivy took Larissa's hand in hers. "I cannot ask you to endure Sir Randall's presence if you do not wish it."

"Sir Randall and I may not like one another, but we find our mutual disharmony an acceptable state and we contrive."

"Do you? How practical of you both."

"I plan on meeting Lord Fenton Harding once we arrive, and Sir Randall, Lady Dorothea Brookhurst."

"How clever of you," Ivy gasped. "Do you find Lord Fenton agreeable, dear?"

Larissa smiled knowingly. "Let's just say I am very interested in furthering our relationship."

Colored lanterns strung from the trees swayed in the gentle breeze, dotting the gardens at Vauxhall. Music with no apparent source laced the air. Larissa felt a sense of excitement drawing her in. When Larissa looked up, Sir Randall had gone and in his place stood Lord Fenton.

Lord Fenton wore a light blue jacket and light-colored pantaloons, a conservative selection. Sir Randall had chosen to wear a fawn-colored jacket with velvet lapels, cream breeches, and Hessians.

"Would you mind if we abandoned you, so I could take your aunt to my box for refreshment?" Rushton asked.

"Not at all," Larissa answered. In fact, she was looking forward to wandering the park at the side of Lord Fenton.

"You are, of course, welcome to join us," the earl added in equitable tones.

"Perhaps later, then." Larissa looked with longing toward Lord Fenton. "It is such a lovely night. I do wish to see the gardens."

"I shall keep a keen eye on Miss Larissa," Lord Fenton promised, placing a protective hand over hers. Ivy nodded, giving her approval. "She shall be quite safe with me."

Larissa flashed a smile at Lord Fenton. Of that, she was quite sure. Lord Fenton had not gone so far as to try to press her hand.

Tonight this would change. If Lord Fenton would not

be brought to kiss her, she would kiss him. She knew there were many men who stole kisses from unsuspecting maidens. She would be the first she knew of to steal a kiss from an unsuspecting man.

"What would you like to see?" Lord Fenton gave one of his dazzling smiles. "What about the rotunda? It's very beautiful. Music, mirrors, crystal chandeliers and paintings. It is a delight for the eyes and ears."

Larissa returned his smile with mischievous intent. "I think it's a nice place to begin," she replied, holding tightly onto her shawl. He led her away from the grove.

The path took them by the wood and iron triumphal arches. Larissa looked at the people strolling along the intersecting crossing walks. Beyond the unevenly lit areas lay the dark walkways, where the lanterns were few and far between. That was the place her aunt had warned her about.

The dark walk, she thought. If only she could somehow convince Lord Fenton to follow her. Before the night was done, she intended to do just that.

Timing would be critical. Lord Fenton could easily outrun her if she decided to make a dash. She needed to wait until he was occupied to gain a suitable head start.

The opportunity presented itself a mere hour later, after visiting the rotunda, the exotic colonnades, and the cascade. They were fortunate to discover an unoccupied bench on which to sit and rest, which Lord Fenton insisted she needed.

"I say, there is Lord Alversly. I haven't seen him in an age."

"Why don't you pay your respects to him," she suggested.

"I'm still feeling fatigued. I'd like to sit here and rest a bit." Larissa smoothed the folds of her skirts on her lap, hoping to look as if she were settling to stay for the duration.

Lord Fenton looked shocked by her idea. "I believe it would be highly unsuitable to subject you to man-talk. Yet, I couldn't possibly leave you," he replied. She suspected he was insulted that she should dare ask him to abandon her. "However," he pondered, reconsidering, "I wanted to have a word with him."

Larissa smiled, attesting to her sincerity. "Please go. I shall wait right here, on this very spot."

Fenton was clearly torn about what to do. After a brief deliberation, he gave in, still obviously undecided. "I shan't be more than a moment." He sketched a bow and legged it to Lord Alversly.

Larissa waited until he was deep into conversation before she hiked her skirts around her ankles and dashed off toward the far temple. Out of breath by the time she reached the steps, Larissa turned backed to see if Fenton had noticed. He hadn't. She climbed to the top and waited, never taking her eyes from him.

Larissa watched Lord Fenton glance at the bench where he had left her, then around the area, looking for her. After their eyes had met, she ran into the temple, taking the steps down the other side and onto the path beyond, plunging into the darkness. She pulled her shawl tight around her shoulders and took cover between some bushes.

Larissa watched Fenton appear. He glanced around from the elevated vantage point of the steps, looking for her. He moved from the lit area near the temple onto the remote path. She waited until he traveled deeper onto the darkened walk, closer to where she crouched tucked between the surrounding hedges in wait. She realized her weeks of eager anticipation were about to come to an end in only a few moments.

Someone coming from the light would find it difficult to see. Her eyes had already become accustomed to the dark. While her victim's eyes were adjusting, it was time to act.

In a few quick steps, Larissa moved from between the shrubbery into the open. Approaching from behind, she stepped in front of Fenton. Her shawl slipped from her shoulders when she reached up and pulled his head down to hers. Her lips found his.

This was not how Sir Randall had kissed her. He bestowed upon her a new type of kiss. A lover's kiss. She pressed against him with all the longing that had built up inside her.

It was heavenly. More than she had remembered a kiss should be. She felt the same thrill in addition to a closeness and a desire to lose herself to the pure pleasure enveloping her. All warm and soft.

Soft as velvet.

Larissa ran her hands up the front of his coat. Under her fingers lay the soft lapels.

Velvet?

She leaped back. "Oh, my heavens . . . you're Sir Randall!"

Chapter Eleven

"Miss Quinn!" Randall exclaimed. Larissa's face took form in the darkness once he heard her voice. "You have a talent for appearing in the most unfortunate of places."

"It is you, sir, who apparently possesses the uncanny timing," Larissa returned. "For it was Lord Fenton I wished to surprise, not you."

"It is Lady Dorothea I seek. We somehow managed to lose one another." He glanced around, squinting to aid his vision.

"If you will be so kind as to release me, I shall be on my way and you can be on yours."

"Indeed. For this is not a place for the innocent, or they should not be innocent for long." Jumping from the bushes and assaulting him was not the act of an innocent. His initial shock had melted into a complacent ardor.

The feel of Larissa's softness, her scent, arose from his dreams and now penetrated his senses. She was like a dream. He caressed her face with a look. "Are you quite sure you wish to leave so soon?" Randall caught Larissa's arm when she turned to leave.

"If you're trying to f-frighten me, it's a rather p-poor attempt," Larissa said, holding her chin high, pulling free from his grasp. She knelt and retrieved her shawl that had slid to the ground.

Randall had the urge to show her exactly what there was to be afraid of. He wanted to pull her into his arms and make her breathless with kisses. Instead he watched her gather her skirts and run down the darkened path into the brightly lit area beyond the temple.

Randall glanced up and stared at the crescent moon, which alone kept him company. Larissa had surprised him. And, unlike Larissa, after the first few seconds he knew exactly who he held in his arms.

In place of the innocence he had sensed on their first kiss, he felt something different. She did not respond as an experienced woman, he felt a hunger, a searching need in her kiss.

Climbing the temple steps, he returned to the gardens. Shrouded under the shadow of an arch stood Lady Dorothea. Randall waved, catching her attention, and made straight for her.

"Where have you been, Sir Randall?" Dorothea cooed.

"Where have I been, indeed. Where have you been? I thought you had disappeared."

"Disappeared? Such nonsense." She laughed. The wide smile faded and her voice grew soft into a whisper. "Are you wanting me, then?"

Randall's eyes shot open in surprise. His breath caught

in his throat, almost choking him. Dorothea could not have meant what Randall thought she meant.

How easy it would be to step behind the triumphal arch with her. Hidden from public view, he could take her into his arms and . . .

He stopped his thoughts from continuing down that lascivious lane. If it were not for his amorous predisposition, no doubt caused by the incident with Larissa, Randall would not have interpreted Dorothea's statement in such a suggestive fashion. How could Randall think a lady such as she was capable of such duplicity?

Larissa collapsed against one of the columns at a distance from where she had discovered Sir Randall. Why, of all people, did it have to be him? She should have known who he was the moment their lips met. The familiar touch of his hand on her cheek, the familiar smell of spice, the familiar feel of his body brought back such pleasant memories.

She walked down the nearest path. After several minutes she arrived at the supper boxes. Larissa pulled up short upon hearing her aunt's voice pierce the surrounding music.

"You want us to marry tomorrow? Why, Rushton, that's impossible."

The earl chuckled. "Not so impossible, my dear. I secured a special license the day I met you." Larissa moved closer and saw Rushton press Ivy's hands within his. "I need not tell you I am not a young man. But I can assure you, the love I feel in my heart for you is not diminished by age." The earl gazed into Ivy's face, his eyes twinkling.

"Oh, Rushton," Ivy blushed. "You are far too hasty in your actions. I cannot think."

"I enjoy it when you do not think," the earl replied, playfully.

"Please . . . I have no doubts for myself. However, I do have Larissa to consider."

"What of her? I find her a lovely girl."

"I can't just leave her alone," Ivy replied.

"Alone? My dear sweet, your Larissa will be much better off. Related to an earl, her chances of a match will increase twofold. Oh yes, a very positive alliance for her. She'll have a new family . . . she'll be far from alone."

Larissa moved back. She hadn't meant to eavesdrop. On the other hand, she felt relieved she had not intruded upon their privacy. Not that the earl's action was unexpected. Sir Randall had warned her of his intentions earlier that night at the opera. But to marry tomorrow? Aunt Ivy was right, it was far too soon.

Stepping farther away from the supper box, Larissa wandered down one of the paths, which delivered her to the stone bench where she had last seen Lord Fenton. She moved toward the unoccupied bench and sat. He still stood there among the very same men. How could that be possible? She was sure he had seen her at the temple before she left for the dark walk. Why had he not followed her?

Not more than a moment after she'd sat, he left his colleagues and was at her side. "It's the funniest thing," he said, raising his quizzing glass and examining her. "For a moment, I thought I saw you standing by that far temple."

"Nonsense." She lied and forced a small laugh. "I haven't dared move from this spot."

"Just as I suspected," he replied, laying his glass to rest on its chain. He offered her his arm. "Shall we join your aunt at the earl's supper box?"

Larissa pulled her shawl tight around her and accepted his arm. "I imagine they might have some happy news to welcome us when we arrive."

"Imagine that," he commented, leading her away.

Larissa decided it would take more than a quizzing glass for Fenton to see what was going on under his own nose. No doubt he would miss Aunt Ivy and the earl smelling thoroughly of April and May.

"Our trunks are loaded onto the coach, and Katherine waits belowstairs," Larissa informed her aunt.

"Very punctual my Katherine," Ivy praised. "I am sorry to do this to you, my dear. I had no intention of marriage when I came to London."

"Do not be sorry." Larissa was very happy for her aunt.

"How my life has changed since you came. I thought we'd have such fun coming to Town. Attending all the parties, balls, and such. Little did I imagine I would be the one to fall in love and marry." She held out her arm and asked, "Fetch my wrap, would you, dear?"

Larissa lifted the blue Norwich shawl from the bed and handed it to her aunt. "In love?"

"Oh yes, my dear." She covered her shoulders. "I should never have remarried unless I was." Her voice grew serious. "I do believe it is time we leave."

Ivy took a last lingering look at her reflection in the pier glass. Her eyes were radiant, almost glowing. She fingered the folds of her gown and ran her hand over her hair, admiring the neat chignon. She regarded the satisfied smile and the high color on her cheeks.

Obviously, blushing was not limited to the young for her aunt flushed the most becoming pink. Some things, Larissa thought, never change.

Arriving at Rushton townhouse, Ivy and Larissa were immediately greeted by the earl.

"There she is now," Rushton announced, rushing to the dowager's side. "My lovely bride." He took both her hands and drew her near, placing a kiss on each cheek. "Have you ever seen any more beautiful?"

"Rushton, shame on you," Ivy sighed. "You put me to the blush, and I am too old for that nonsense."

"Ah, no, my love." He placed a kiss on her hand. "You shall see. Life has just begun for us." Rushton gave an all-encompassing look before announcing, "Let us not waste a moment longer." He released one of her hands and reached out to one side. "Laurie," he called.

The butler appeared, handing the earl a nosegay of white roses with small green ivy threaded through. The earl inhaled its fragrance before presenting the love token to his bride.

"For you, my dear. Ivy for the most delicate Ivy of all."

She accepted the flowers. "Why, thank you, Rushton."

"Let us remove to the blue parlor and proceed." Laurie led the way with Ivy and Larissa following. The clergyman, Rushton, and Sir Randall brought up the rear.

Larissa immediately noticed the parlor was not blue, but yellow. She glanced at the others. No one else seemed to have observed the incongruity, it seemed, except for her. She would certainly not bring up such a trivial fact on such an important day as this.

The clergyman indicated where the bride, groom, and witnesses should stand, then proceeded. The ceremony was short, lasting no more than fifteen minutes followed by a brief celebration.

"I told Larissa I have asked one of your maids, Abby, to attend her since I am taking Katherine with me. I am still concerned about her, though," the new countess confessed to Rushton.

"Did you not send for a chaperone for Larissa?" the earl queried.

"Yes, but Mrs. Rutledge will not arrive until tomorrow."

"It is not even one full day. Surely we can entrust her care to my nephew until then," Rushton suggested.

"But won't that seem odd?"

Rushton sighed and eased into his chair. "My nephew has the most upstanding character, high morals, and sense of what is right of any one I know."

Having Larissa in his care was the last thing Sir Randall wanted as well. Above all, he did not want to compromise his developing romance with Lady Dorothea.

"Not to worry, my dearest," the earl said to his new bride's hand. "Larissa and Randall are connected now. Randall is a gentleman beyond reproach."

"Dash it, Uncle Cyrus, I wish you wouldn't talk about me as if I were not here," Randall grumbled, hoping someone would include him in the conversation.

"Who knows what sort of scoundrel lurks about in the shadows and sits ready to pounce," Ivy said in imaginary horror of fiends and seducers after her niece. "I must check on her." She flustered with this unpleasant talk and left the room.

"Pounce? Scoundrels?" Randall repeated in alarm after the countess left. "I think this is all a bit far-fetched don't you, Uncle?"

"Perhaps, but it shall keep her aunt happy." Rushton sat forward and shook a finger at his nephew. "And I need not remind you, if she's plagued with worry over Larissa's welfare"—the earl took up a coquettish falsetto and did his best imitation of his new wife—"whether she's happy or whether she's safe, I shan't—" He coughed and resumed his normal tone, "We shan't have any kind of bridal trip at all. I hope I don't make myself sound too selfish about all this. I do care about Larissa. She's a fine girl and I won't mind that she'll be moving in with us after the Season. I'm really quite fond of her."

"She's to reside at Rushton Manor?" Randall remarked, outraged.

"Unless she can manage a marriage soon, she will have to." The earl gazed at Randall with a pleading look he had never seen before. "Please say you'll agree. If not for sweet Larissa's sake, then for mine."

Sweet Larissa? The chit had them fooled. All of them. It was clear, at least to Randall, he was the only one who knew what the real Larissa was all about.

"Of course I shall, Uncle. You know all you need do is ask."

"I knew I could count on you." Rushton smiled and clapped his nephew on the back. "Always have. You will, of course, attend to the social obligations I have already accepted in my absence."

"Of course," he agreed. Rushton gave a great roar of laughter, exuding happiness beyond belief and pranced out of the drawing room. Randall had never seen his uncle so happy. His uncle knew Randall would have promised him anything. And what more could there be after taking on the responsibility of watching over Larissa?

It was a momentous undertaking, and perhaps one that only Randall could comprehend. He'd need to keep careful watch on her and on her unrestricted mouth. Those lovely lips could spout the deepest of lies. They could also curl into the most sumptuous of smiles and lay waste to a man's willpower with a single kiss.

Kiss?

He shook the image from his head. What was he thinking? He had Dorothea to consider. What would she think if he spent so much time playing chaperone to this brat?

From out of nowhere Laurie appeared. "It was his lordship's wish I remind you of the approaching events he has informed me you are to attend in his absence."

Randall sighed. There was no escape. He had Larissa to watch over and his uncle's social commitments to keep. In Rushton's absence, the butler would see to it Randall attended.

"All right, Laurie, I'm listening," Randall gave in.

"May I remind you that only a fortnight of the Season remains, sir."

"Thank you, I shall keep that in mind." That didn't make the burden any easier to bear.

"Tomorrow evening, there is a soiree at Lord and Lady Pringle's. The following afternoon at three, the Earl of Westmont is holding a Water Party. That evening, of course, his lordship has vouchers to Almack's."

Randall would have done anything for his uncle. Anything but . . . "I'm not stepping one foot inside that place. I've had enough of its giggling girls and meddlesome marriage mamas to last me years on end. I don't care what Uncle Cyrus says, I'll not be attending that melee."

"My lord understands your dislike of the public assembly and has expressed that you need not attend if you do not wish," the butler replied without reacting to Randall's emotional rebuff.

"Oh? Well." Randall felt a bit embarrassed at his outburst, but quickly composed himself. "Then I do not wish to attend."

The social engagements would last only until tomorrow. After that, the chaperone would arrive and Randall's responsibility to Larissa would be over.

If nothing else, there was an end in sight.

Chapter Twelve

When Larissa awoke from her afternoon rest, the townhouse that had at first felt so welcoming when she arrived by her aunt's side seemed strange and intimidating.

She would prefer to be all alone than alone with Sir Randall.

Where was Sir Randall? Larissa moved down the main hall, her sweeping gaze alert for his evidence.

"May I be of assistance, Miss?"

Larissa gasped and spun around. She clutched her throat in fright. "Oh, it's you," she said. "Laurie, is it not?"

"Yes, Miss."

"I was wondering if Sir Randall was about."

"No, miss. Sir Randall has gone out." The news was music to her ears. "Shall I have Mrs. Drum bring tea into the parlor?"

"Yes, Laurie. That would be quite nice."

Larissa settled onto the sofa in the front parlor, followed

minutes later by the swift-moving Mrs. Drum, the house-keeper, who, to all appearances, lived up to her name. The woman was round, wide, and the top of her hat was flat.

"It's so splendid to have ladies about the house." Mrs. Drum set out a plate and napkin for Larissa and poured a cup of tea. "Since the first Countess of Rushton passed on, there have not been any ladies in the house." She rattled on, "His lordship had hardly spent anytime in Town at all."

Larissa had passed the cakes and opted for tea only. She was grateful for the housekeeper's talkative nature, for it kept her from feeling so alone. Larissa suspected that was one of the reasons the earl kept her.

"Now, not only has his lordship come to stay with his nephew, but there are two ladies about. Not to mention a new countess!"

"And may I say that no one is more pleased than I." It was Sir Randall's baritone that interrupted the coze.

Larissa's cup skittered on its saucer, clinking about in the most horrific manner.

"Will you be having tea, Sir Randall?" Mrs. Drum had a cup ready for him.

"Please, Mrs. Drum."

Larissa hadn't heard Sir Randall enter the room, much less climb the stairs. She really needed to pay closer attention to the goings-on around her.

"Are you quite well?" he asked Larissa. She had hoped he hadn't noticed her nervousness with the china when he entered.

"Yes, thank you. Quite," she replied in a curt manner. "Quite well. Why ever would you think not?"

With tea in hand, Sir Randall sat in the adjacent chair. "If I may hazard a guess." He regarded her from beneath a raised brow. "I should say you feel quite peculiar about sneaking up on me last night at Vauxhall Gardens."

Larissa took great offense at his reminder of such an indiscretion. "I did not sneak up on you. I've already explained that it was a mistake."

"As you say, then. However, if you are having second thoughts about us . . ." He smiled, teasing.

"Us?" Larissa repeated in alarm. Larissa sincerely hoped he was teasing. "There is no *us* to consider."

"All alone in this big house." Sir Randall's gaze roamed about the expansive room. "Perhaps it is *I* who should be wary of being alone with you. After all, you were the one who—"

"Please, Sir Randall. Pray you forget any notion of that sort. As you well know, I only seek the attentions of Lord Fenton," she said in hauteur.

"And I, as *you* well know, only seek the attentions of Lady Dorothea. After spending a good portion of the afternoon in her company, I can assure you she has *my* complete attention. So there is nothing at all to worry about, is there?"

"No, I suppose there isn't. We do understand one another then?"

"Perfectly."

With that Larissa felt confident enough to relax and break into a smile. "Good."

At the Pringles' soiree that night, Larissa left the green parlor on the arm of Lord Fenton. She erupted into one spasm after another of laughter, knowing full well such a display was not considered the proper demeanor of a lady. Lord Fenton was not the least bit helpful with regaining her composure. He roared in hysterics, causing her to continue despite the disapproving glances from the other guests. It was just outside the parlor when they happened upon Sir Randall, who took particular notice of their joyous condition. The laughter was contagious, Larissa noticed, causing a smile to erupt on Sir Randall's normally somber face.

"May I ask what you find so humorous?"

"Sir Randall," Lord Fenton managed, catching his breath and slowly exhaled. "We had the most delightful time playing a parlor game."

"A game?"

"Was it 'Questions and Commands' or 'Cross Purposes and Crooked Answers' we were playing?"

"'Cross Purposes and Crooked Answers,'" Larissa confirmed.

"One thinks of games as being for children. But, I say, when played with a dozen or so adults it is ripping good fun. Was it not?"

"Very." Larissa wiped the remaining tears from her eyes.

"I think I've hurt myself, laughing so hard." Lord Fenton ran his hand down his green-striped waistcoat and patted his midsection.

"That is a shame," Sir Randall replied. He did not sound the least bit sorry.

"Do let me fetch some lemonade for us," Lord Fenton offered.

"Would you?" Larissa gave Lord Fenton an adoring gaze. "I would be ever so grateful."

"Would you mind, Sir Randall, keeping an eye on Miss Larissa?"

"I can hardly refuse," he said with a smile.

"I shall be back in a thrice, then." Lord Fenton paddled out of the room.

And after Lord Fenton had left Sir Randall mumbled, "I have already promised to do as much."

Larissa felt quite at ease, even in Sir Randall's company.

"Are you having a pleasant evening?" Sir Randall queried in ever so nice a tone, one that Larissa had never before heard directed at her.

"Yes, very. And you, Sir Randall? How goes it with you?"

"It goes very well, thank you," he said in satisfaction.

"I'm sure you have Lady Dorothea to thank, surely, not me." His smile reassured her she was correct on both counts. "By the bye, where is Lady Dorothea?"

"Have no fear, she shall return momentarily."

They stood quietly for a moment. "Isn't life funny, Sir Randall?" Larissa prattled on, encompassing the concept of grander schemes.

"In what way is that, pray tell?"

"You and I for example." She took his bewildered expression as the perfect reason to continue. "Consider the way we met and our unusual acquaintance. One would think we would be at daggers drawn. But just look at us." She gestured to their elegant, peaceful surroundings. "Here we stand, now related, albeit only just recently, behaving quite civilly, near to genuine affection, I should think, and resting in the boughs of another. Not *with* one another, you understand," she clarified.

"Of course." A shallow nod forgave her verbal faux pas. "*Are* you taken with Lord Fenton?"

"Why, of course I am," she stated, insulted that he should even ask. Wasn't it obvious? "He is like none other."

"I do believe you have the right of it."

"And Lady Dorothea?"

Sir Randall smiled. "I believe she is without equal."

Larissa sensed affection in his voice. He did care for Lady Dorothea.

"Miss Quinn, Sir Randall," Sir Thomas White acknowledged the pair when he stepped between them in the midst of his jaunt across the room. Dressed in evening finery, Sir Thomas paused and made a hasty but elegant leg.

"Sir Thomas," Larissa and Sir Randall chorused.

"A pleasant evening to you both," was his gracious reply before he continued on his way.

"My," Larissa sighed. "He *was* in a hurry."

"Apparently," Sir Randall drawled.

"I say," Lord Fenton exclaimed, lifting his arms to hold the lemonade glasses out of the hazardous path of the retreating Sir Thomas, avoiding a near miss. "Let's do find somewhere to sit. Such a crush, don't you know. It would be such a shame if this should spill onto that fine frock of yours." He and Larissa left Sir Randall and found a place to sit.

A few moments later, Lady Dorothea returned to Randall's side. Randall felt his heart begin to pound at the sight of her. He could not get over Dorothea's ethereal presence. She seemed to float on air, her steps were so light.

"The heat is becoming quite unbearable." She opened her fan and coaxed the air to move. "Would you mind if we took a turn about the garden?"

"Not at all." Randall led her through the crowded room to the rear gardens. The air was cool and fresh. From high above, the moon surrounded them with a dim pool of moonlight.

Dorothea stopped and turned to face Randall. Her arms were bare and she allowed the fan to dangle from her wrist.

"Where are your gloves?" Randall looked to either side of her.

"It is so very warm. I just want them off for a moment."

"Where are they? Where did you put them?" Randall moved her skirts, causing his hands to brush about her legs. Something was still not right.

She let out a laugh that was more like a string of musical notes. "What are you doing?"

"I'm trying to discern where you've placed your gloves. Either you dabble in magic or you've a concealed pocket."

Dorothea trailed the tip of her finger along his jaw to his chin and gave him a playful smile. "Wouldn't you like to know?" She spun, taking a step away from him and placed her fan between them. Drawing it open, she allowed Randall time to study the lowering of her full lashes and the pursing of her delicious lips. "Randall. May I be so bold as to call you Randall?"

"Nothing would make me happier," he said. Those brilliant blue eyes looked up at him. Her lips widened into a breathtaking smile.

"Nothing?" Her eyebrows lifted. "I did have one other thought that might please you."

"Really?" There was almost nothing he could deny her when she displayed that enchanting smile. He felt as if he were under a magic spell she wove by moonlight. "And what would that be?"

"We do rub along well together, don't you think?"

"Exceedingly well," he said, still studying her tempting mouth and taking her hand. As the days passed, he was spending more and more time with Dorothea. And more and more he enjoyed her company.

"Then you will speak to Maman about paying your addresses, then?"

He was beginning to think along the lines of marriage himself. And Dorothea was the lady he had in mind. Although he did not yet feel quite ready to take the step, he did not object to her raising the subject.

"I would not be averse to speaking to your mother about you." A grin crept over Randall's lips and he placed a lingering kiss upon her bare hand. "I will do so at the most opportune moment."

If the night at Vauxhall Gardens did not gain her Fenton's kiss, Larissa wondered if tonight would. She felt hesitant about making a second attempt, since the results of the first had not been exactly what she had planned.

She scanned the room for Sir Randall. The last thing she wanted was a repeat of last night—not that she did not enjoy kissing him. It was she who had initiated the kiss, to be sure. For the few seconds it had lasted, it seemed to her Sir Randall had returned the kiss, thus encouraging her. But of course she could be wrong. Knowing the way he felt about her, why on earth would he want to encourage her?

Larissa felt that Lord Fenton was by far more appealing than the previous three gentlemen she had met during the Season—Mr. Wesley Tyson, the Right Honorable Robert Egerton, or Mr. Donald Sinclair. Those men she had not wanted to kiss, she did not feel for them as she did for Lord Fenton. After taking his arm, they strolled out in the small garden. He slowed their pace to nearly a standstill.

"You look most becoming when put to the blush, Miss Larissa."

She raised her hand to her cheek. "Am I blushing?" Little did Fenton know it was Sir Randall of whom she thought, and the similar circumstances of the previous night gave rise to her color. It was her ardent hope that when Fenton held her she would not think of Sir Randall.

Lord Fenton's hand tightened over hers in silent communication, telling her not to flee—the moment was close at hand. A silent breeze ruffled a lock of hair on his forehead. It gave the slightest rakishness to his otherwise perfect appearance.

As they reached the farthest point in the garden behind the Pringles' townhouse, they stopped. "I hope to tell you how I feel about you, Miss Larissa," he said. He drew her into his arms and Larissa leaned into him, hoping he would be a man, take the lead, and continue.

Lord Fenton took hold of Larissa's forearm and turned

it gently behind her back, propelling her closer to him. His long finger trailed from her chin along her jaw and he took his time to study her face before their long-anticipated kiss. But he did not kiss her.

This was not Larissa's only disappointment. Where was the melting she expected to carry her away? The tingling sensations that coursed through her body?

Fenton said something, but Larissa hadn't been listening. She felt confused, too distracted by what she was not feeling.

"It's all right, then?" She heard him say.

"Oh, yes," Larissa replied. "Of course." She didn't know to what Fenton referred. Concentrating on more important matters, she still did not understand what had gone wrong.

Once again, Lord Fenton settled Larissa's hand in the crook of his arm and again placed his hand protectively over the top of hers, continuing their stroll to the house.

Larissa sat at her dressing table, brushed her hair and looked into the glass, oblivious of her reflection. The soiree had been splendid. She adored Lord Fenton, but he did not kiss her as she had wished and on the whole left her feeling less than warm. She replaced her brush on the table and slid into bed. Laying her head on the pillow, she continued to ponder the aftereffects of Fenton's show of affection.

She closed her eyes, praying sleep would carry her into a glorious dream filled with blissful embraces and smoldering kisses. Instead, she lay awake with every indication sleep would not overtake her soon.

Larissa threw back the covers as a restless feeling urged her to her feet. She needed answers to the questions that continued to plague her. Donning her wrapper, Larissa left her room and went belowstairs. She peered into the library. There, facing the blazing hearth, sat Sir Randall.

"I do beg your pardon." Larissa stood at the doorway. "Please forgive my appearance." She glanced down at herself and clutched the front of her garment, holding it close.

The sight of her undress did not bother him. He had seen her this way, and in far more intimate surroundings. Randall couldn't help but think of the night that threw them together. He then reminded himself he was to watch out *for* her, not watch her.

"I fear I am having difficulty falling asleep. I thought I might come down for something to read," she said. She was reserved and shy, like the Larissa he had once known, the young woman he knew before London. "As you are here, perhaps I might speak to you a moment."

"Why, yes of course," he replied. What could possibly be of so grave a matter? Larissa appeared agitated, a state Randall had not seen before. He grew curious.

"I'm not sure how to go about this or if you are the correct person I should approach on this matter." She became very still.

"Please sit down," he instructed. Larissa perched on the edge of the sofa. "If this is such an unpleasant matter, why don't you come directly to the point then."

Larissa didn't look disturbed as much as she seemed preoccupied. She never looked up to meet his gaze. She sat silent for a moment before starting. "I tried to persuade Lord Fenton to kiss me tonight."

"What?" Randall shot forward, gripping the arms of his chair. How would she allow that whey-faced cawker such liberties?

"I find him quite agreeable," she said in all honesty. "I thought I might enjoy kissing him."

"And you didn't?" It almost pleased Randall to hear her admit it.

"But we never did kiss, not really. I had such hope for him." She sighed, disappointed. "He took me in his arms and . . . it wasn't at all similar to when you kissed me."

Randall felt his eyes grow wide. "Is this what it's all about, then? Vauxhall Gardens? I must remind you that—"

"I thought that when a man kissed a woman it should feel—" She still could not meet his gaze, and with good reason. Such an unseemly topic of conversation between the sexes.

"Any real gentleman would not take advantage of a lady," Randall mumbled none too quietly.

"Nor would any lady put herself in that position if she did not wish him to attempt such a maneuver." Larissa did meet his eyes for a brief moment. "If I am to understand correctly."

"Exactly how many men have you gone about taking this action?" Randall reeled in disbelief.

"It is not *every* gentleman. Aunt Ivy says that one must pick and choose. So I have entertained many men during the early part of my Season and decided that I would not have any of them."

"Exactly—" He cleared his throat. "Exactly how many men have you turned away?"

"A few," she answered, then reconsidered. "Perhaps several more than that." Larissa caught her bottom lip with her teeth. She ticked off her fingers, turning her eyes toward the ceiling in contemplation. "I should think not more than . . ."

"Good lord!" Randall sighed in exasperation and rubbed his now throbbing forehead.

"I believe my standards must be quite high for me to find so many men unsatisfactory." She began to list them. "Sir Thomas White was just before Lord Fenton . . ."

"Please—" He silenced her with a raised hand. "No names. Nor do I wish to hear any details. You cannot play fast and loose with every gentleman that comes along."

"It is only Lord Fenton I wished to kiss me, not any of the others," she said in exasperation to Randall, as if he were the one who had done something wrong.

"I cannot tell you how reassuring that is. I'm sure your aunt will have plenty to say about this when she returns," he warned. "Do remember to tell her all this happened *before* you were left in my care."

"I'm afraid I don't understand why you're so upset."

"Upset?" Randall scoffed. Perhaps it was not Larissa's fault as much as it was her aunt's. To encourage her niece to seek the attention of so many men was irresponsible—*maddening*—and if he weren't so concerned perhaps it would not bother him to this extent.

His uncle's new countess-bride should have known better than to instruct Larissa to cast out so many lures. It was not in the best interests of the girl. Not in her best interests at all.

He leaned back in his chair and rubbed the piercing ache in the center of his forehead. Randall's first impulse was to go out for some fresh air. The next was to have a strong drink.

Chapter Thirteen

Randall found a glass waiting for him at Brook's. Easing into one of the many leather wingback chairs, he swallowed the remainder of the brandy and ordered another.

Uncle Cyrus and his new bride had not been gone half a day before Randall had lost control. Lost it? He never had it. He was surrounded by forward females. Larissa had not been the only one. There had also been Lady Dorothea earlier this evening.

How had he let himself get talked into speaking to her mother? He was attracted to Dorothea. He had been thinking about marriage, but paying his addresses—now that he had a chance to think about it . . . he wasn't sure now was the time. Especially since it was at her request. He didn't consider it proper behavior for a lady.

Ladies did not suggest when it was time for their beaus to ask for their hand and ladies did not go around kissing gentlemen. It was the gentlemen who were to decide when to speak to the ladies' parents and when to initiate the kiss, and no real gentleman would kiss a lady unless he had honorable intentions.

Randall knew how delightfully she kissed. He smiled into his glass and took a deep drink. He drummed his fingers. Why in heaven's name hadn't her aunt taught the chit some restraint?

"Look, Dalton, it's a celebration!" Sir Thomas White peered around Randall's chair.

"If we're celebrating, then why does Trent look so miserable?" Oliver groaned.

"Must be a woman," Sir Thomas mused. He would surely be the one to know about troubles caused by women.

A raunchy gurgle came from Oliver. From the look and smell of them, Randall decided they were already well into their cups.

"Come on, Trent," Sir Thomas said. He tugged the lace at his wrists, adjusting the lengths. "Oliver and I are off to find some entertainment." They gave a bawdy laugh.

"No. You two go on ahead."

"Thomas, this one's not plagued by women. He's got trouble with only one woman," Oliver pointed out to his friend.

"I know precisely the one. She's a blessed beauty, that one is," Sir Thomas taunted. "Don't think we don't know you've singled her out."

"You can keep your trap shut, if you please," Randall spat back. Larissa had already mentioned her brief acquaintance with Sir Thomas.

"You might as well know, Trent. No man's safe with her. She'll wind a man around her little finger and grab hold of him by his vitals. Leads him around that way. Gets you to do anything. You'd best watch yourself."

"Come now, Thomas," Oliver urged. "The ladies will be wondering what's been keeping us. We'd best be on our way."

The following afternoon, the sun was shining in glorious celebration of a fine London summer's day. A very nice day for the barge party. The Rushton coach delivered Randall and Larissa close to the launching area. The guests arriving before them had set the precedent of strolling along the small worn path by the river's edge.

The immense barge sat at the pier. Green and yellow drapes decorated the railings. A refreshment table sat midship under an enormous awning. An orchestra shared the awning, facing the rear of the craft. If one stood at one end, surely they could not see someone standing at the other.

A finer day to set sail could not be imagined. The wind was calm, yet strong enough to cause the yellow awning to billow and sag with the gentle breeze. Today the barge would glide smoothly over the water. Larissa opened her parasol and rested it upon her shoulder.

She noticed Sir Randall eyeing the crowd. Looking for Lady Dorothea no doubt. She followed his example and made her own search for Lord Fenton. Larissa spotted Fenton by the splendor of his dress, ever so handsome in his bottle green coat, canary breeches, and Hessians.

"I am come," he announced and greeted one and all with a great flourish. "Delighted, as always, Miss Larissa." His voice held a richness she had not noticed before.

"Hard-ing," Sir Randall drawled, in his usual tolerant tone.

Sir Randall was probably jealous of Fenton's fine fashion sense or his elegant stature. Larissa glanced at the yellow-and-green-decorated barge and back again at Fenton.

"How ever did you know, Lord Fenton?"

Fenton mimicked Larissa's gesture, glancing at the barge and down at his similarly colored canary and green clothes. "What an amazing coincidence." He chuckled. "Would you care to take a short stroll toward the bow?"

Larissa sensed his wish to be alone with her, away from the disapproving Sir Randall. "I would, let's," she agreed.

"If you will be so kind as to excuse us," Fenton said to Sir Randall.

"Of course," Sir Randall replied.

Fenton led Larissa down the narrow path toward the barge at the water's edge.

"Sir Randall!" Lady Brookhurst's voice penetrated through the bustle of carriages and abounding noise of the outdoors. "There you are." She waved her lace handkerchief to catch his attention before heading in his direction.

"Lady Brookhurst," Randall bowed, accepting her hand. "Lady Dorothea," he said with equal formality.

"I see Lady Sefton," Lady Brookhurst trilled. "You will excuse me won't you, dear?"

"Yes, Maman. I shan't leave Sir Randall's side." Dorothea's coy side glance alluded to more than a demure attitude.

Randall did not know if Lady Brookhurst's absence was planned or not on her part. He had noticed she always seemed to leave them alone at the most opportune moments.

"Would you not like to walk the path before we board?" Dorothea asked.

"I thought I might speak to you alone for a moment," Randall whispered to Dorothea.

"Of course," she cooed, displaying a smile which in other circumstances might charm him, but had no such effect this time. They stepped away from the pier and the other guests.

After finding a natural screen of tall hedges, Dorothea spun to face him. "Are you going to kiss me?" She batted her wide eyes while a wicked smile crossed her face.

Although he felt hesitant to do so, Randall leaned forward and bent his head, bringing his lips near hers. She arched her back, molding herself to his body.

He recognized the well-practiced form. This was not the posture of a woman who lacked experience. Randall froze and held her by her shoulders at a distance and took a step back. If he had any doubts about his decision to break off with her before, this action sealed her fate.

"Aren't you going to kiss me?" she asked. Her innocent act was exactly that, he realized. An act.

"I think not," he said in formal tones. "Also, I think I will not be speaking to your mother."

"What?" Dorothea shrieked, clutching two fistfuls of skirt. "You promised!"

"No, I don't believe that's entirely the truth of the matter," he corrected her.

"There's someone else, isn't there? I want to know who she is." Dorothea stomped, tamping the dirt beneath her feet. "Who is she!"

You'd best watch yourself. Sir Thomas' words rang

through his head. It was not Larissa Quinn he had been speaking of last night. It must have been Lady Dorothea Brookhurst. Was she not using the wiles they spoke of to ensnare him?

Randall tore himself away from Dorothea's scene and headed for the barge.

He felt the ornate barge rock beneath his feet with every step. Guests strolled to and fro as if they occupied the finest drawing room in London instead of floating on the Thames.

Randall suspected something was not quite right. When the aroma of food drifted in his direction, it became increasingly clear the problem originated in his stomach. Erupted might be a more accurate description. He made a dash for the side railing.

In his hurry, Randall charged between Lord Langley and Sir Thomas White, without begging their pardon, sending them tumbling in opposite directions. Randall's last effort bowled over another man, who did not take kindly to his abrupt dislocation.

"What's all this?" he cried out, catching his balance and glaring at Randall.

Randall made it in time to cascade into the water. He knew it was the result of last night's drink. His digestive tract had never dealt well with alcohol and the precarious nature of the barge must have added to his stomach's upset. Regaining his balance, Randall took the proffered dampened cloth napkin dangling from the fingers of his friend Sir Thomas White.

"Too late to abandon ship now, old man. We've just gone to sea." Sir Thomas drawled, amused. "Will you live?"

Randall applied the cool linen to his upper lip and sweat-beaded forehead. "I sincerely hope not." He leaned against the railing, closed his eyes and drew a measured breath.

"Ah, Sir Randall—Trent, is it? Had it in mind that your name was Quid or Quint or some other nonsense." A well-to-do gentleman pried Randall's arm from the railing and pumped it in greeting. "Like the way you put the termagant in her place."

"I beg your pardon?" A confused Randall racked his brain for recognition. "Excuse me, sir. I don't believe we have been introduced."

"Shared a coach to Oxford with you some months ago. I might have been in my cups, but I ain't blind. Quite a display you put on for that nosy fishwife."

Randall felt a jolt of shock hit, numbing him.

"Shouldn't have come aboard. As I remember, you suffer from *mal de mer*, if I'm not mistaken. That's what I recall your wife saying."

"My wife?" Randall repeated in confusion.

"Wife?" Sir Thomas echoed with renewed interest.

"I can see you're trying your best to stay on her good side, what? Smart man." The man winked and elbowed Sir Thomas. "By the bye, where is your lovely bride?" He smiled and looked around, revealing a gold-capped front tooth.

Randall began to feel his stomach lurch. Only this time, it was a sinking feeling.

"He's a brave man, Sir Thomas." The well-dressed stranger remarked about Randall. "Ah, there she is now." He pointed across the barge. "I shall pay my respects and tell her not to torture you so and to take you ashore at once." With that, the stout man strolled off.

"Who is he?" Randall gasped, when he was certain he could not be heard.

"That man," Sir Thomas mused, "is Sir Purvis Archwald. He has made himself indispensable to His Royal Highness, the Duke of Clarence. The Duke had Sir Purvis knighted."

"What on earth was he doing on a public coach?"

"Same as you, I imagine," Sir Thomas surmised. "Had to get home. He's a nice allowance, but he's not what you'd call plump in the pockets."

Randall watched Sir Purvis move to the port side of the boat, disappearing into the crowd, which graciously parted to allow him passage.

"How delightful to see you again, Lady Trent. I'm afraid we've spent time traveling together and yet have not had a proper introduction. I am Sir Purvis Archwald." He made a shallow bow. "At your service."

What did he say? Larissa had not uttered a reply. Glancing around she could see heads drawing together, hear whispers she could not decipher. She turned in time to see Lord Fenton's reaction when word reached him. Fenton went pale. The glasses of punch he carried shook in his hand, spilling the contents. Larissa felt her face grow warm, and pressed her hands to her cheek.

"Lady Trent, have I said something wrong?" Sir Purvis glanced around for confirmation. He seemed to miss the gawking gazes of those few who stood around them and continued. "You know, your husband is one of the most outrageous men I've met." He chuckled and was the only one doing so at the moment. "Oh, yes. Quite the sense of humor, your husband has."

Larissa endured the remainder of his monologue in silence.

Lord Fenton waited until Sir Purvis left before returning to Larissa's side

"Married?" Lord Fenton growled. He stared at Larissa, his eyes narrowing into slits.

"It's not true," she cried.

"Who is he?" Fenton took Larissa roughly by an arm, looking for someone who took more than a casual interest in observing them. "Are you married to some social oddity who need hide himself from public view? Some eccentric elderly earl, perhaps?"

"No," Larissa refuted. "That's not the way it is at all." She wanted to explain, but how could she? She wasn't sure what was happening herself. Who was that man? He had called her Lady Trent, meaning Sir Randall must be her husband.

"Why didn't you just reject my offer last night?"

"Last night?" Larissa had no idea to what he was referring. Had he offered for her? How could she have missed that?

"You knew I wanted to marry you." A snide, lopsided smile, an expression Larissa had never seen, spread over Fenton's lips. She saw a disturbing glint in his eyes. And for the first time he frightened her.

She was afraid of kind, polite Lord Fenton. Fenton, who never made an improper move. Fenton, who always kept her welfare in mind. Fenton, who now was pulling her about roughly by her arm.

"How could you allow me to go on so? Was it as much of a joke to you as it was to your husband? To watch some lowly third son of a duke make a demmed fool of himself?"

Larissa pried at his fingers. "Please, Fenton, you're hurting me."

He shoved her toward the railing and paced an arc around her. She hoped the water-worthy craft's deck would not buckle under his heavy, hammering steps.

"I'm one of the most sought-after men in Society. Do you realize how many young women set out traps for me?"

"Then I trust you will have no trouble finding another," she said in realization. Larissa no longer wanted him. Then, she realized in that moment that she had never really wanted him.

"I had wished to marry you." He glared at her. "Why would you do this to me?"

"I am afraid any explanation I could give would prove unsatisfactory."

"I imagine it would. Suffice it to say, I shan't want anything to do with you again," Fenton's voice sounded odd, distant, emotionless.

Tears pooled in Larissa's eyes. "I quite understand."

"If you will *pardon me*," Fenton performed an exquisite leg, "I shall take leave of you now."

Still pressing the linen to his mouth, Randall steadied himself on Sir Thomas' shoulder.

"Look there." Sir Thomas gestured with his head to the very lovely, very angry Lady Dorothea.

Randall saw Dorothea and Lady Brookhurst under the awning.

"Married!" Dorothea's voice carried on the wind. She met his gaze and glared daggers at him. Her reaction to the circulating rumor was not at all the picture of loveliness Randall was accustomed to seeing. She broke off her stare and fell into her mother's arms. "He used me, Maman," she sobbed.

Randall heard Sir Thomas turn away and snicker. "I'm afraid you're in for it, my man." He gave Randall a clap on the arm and left.

From years of experience, Randall knew Sir Thomas was right when it came to the ladies. A slight uneasiness came over him. He wondered what it was he was *in* for. Bracing himself with both hands on the railing, Randall once again faced forward. Then he saw her.

With new set composure and her head held high, Dorothea strolled toward Randall. "You'll be sorry for doing this to me," she threatened and stalked away.

He knew she would not be speaking to him again. It was really over between them. When Randall thought the trip could not get any worse, he saw Larissa heading in his direction.

Chapter Fourteen

"Would you be so kind as to tell me—"

"Please," he shushed Larissa and led her toward the great awning, now deserted, in the center of the boat. The faces of the servants remained impassive, unaffected by the latest gossip sweeping the vessel.

"I need a drink." Randall wished he could order a whiskey. The strongest drink he could find was punch. He eyed the fury that clouded Larissa's usual lovely visage and added, "I trust you are in need of one as well." He drained the first glass and offered the second to her.

"I don't want that." She pushed the glass away.

"Well, best not let it go to waste, then." He downed the contents of her glass. Larissa's horror, which Randall saw depicted in her eyes, replaced the anger of only minutes before.

He held his eyes closed for a few moments and prayed

for calm. "Now, you may continue," he prompted. "But quietly, please."

Larissa glanced around her and saw no one. She leaned closer to Randall.

"Who is that Sir Purvis Archwald?" she demanded, her eyes boring into him. "He cannot possibly be who I think he is."

"And why not?" Randall was certain she also remembered Sir Purvis as the foxed passenger in the coach to Oxford.

"But really? The man was unconscious."

"Obviously not as unconscious as we had thought. Shall we get some fresh air?" Randall offered Larissa his arm. He ignored her protest, linked her arm with his, and held her hand in the crook of his arm.

Larissa struggled to free herself from Randall's hold, but to no avail. "Do you mind? I wish you wouldn't force yourself upon me."

"Have you noticed we seem to be very much alone?"

"Alone? What do you mean, alone? The boat is filled with guests." The puzzled expression grew once she noticed their isolation. They were seemingly quite alone aboard this large water vessel. "Where is . . . where has everyone gone?"

"They're about, I can assure you," Randall softened his voice. "Watching every move we make."

Larissa's eyes widened.

"You should show some enthusiasm," he prompted.

"Why?"

"You do share the company of your new husband." He

performed a dazzling smile, placing himself on display for all who cared to see.

"You're as bad as they are." Larissa glanced around, imagining the guests whispering and chuckling at her expense. "You cannot take all this seriously."

"We are as good as wed in the eyes of Society," he assured her.

"But Society rumors do not a marriage make," she retorted.

"How true, how true. Who do you think the members of Society are going to believe, Sir Purvis, confidant of the Duke of Clarence, or us?"

"Will you not even try to deny it?"

"How can I?" Sir Randall shrugged in defeat. "Call every member of the *ton* a liar? I think not. The thing is as well as done. In an hour, word will have traveled up and down the Thames and by tonight all of London will know. We'd look the fool to deny it."

Larissa hadn't realized. Was High Society so powerful? From the look on Sir Randall's face, she assumed it was, for he would not lift a finger to fight it.

"Whatever are we to do?"

Sir Randall stared at Larissa, smiled that disarming smile of his, and said, "We continue to pretend we are married."

His words startled her. How far would he go to perpetuate this lie? He certainly could not compare this circumstance with the one at The Blue Boar Inn. Spending one night at an obscure posting house and prolonging the pretense of marriage in London were two entirely different matters. In the country, only a few people had known of their nonexistent nuptials. How unfortunate for them one of those passengers happened to be Sir Purvis Archwald.

Disembarking now was out of the question. Larissa sat with Sir Randall, isolated, on display under the scrutiny of the other guests. She and Sir Randall on one side of the craft and the remainder of the guests on the other, all but pointing at the two of them.

"I do so wish to put on a convincing show," Sir Randall informed her.

"What on earth for?" Larissa could see Sir Randall's eyes linger, not on her, but past her. "What is it? What are you looking at?

Sir Randall laid his hand along her neck and jaw, preventing her head from turning. "It's Lord Langleigh and the Earl of Westmont," he whispered.

"But, what if they . . ." she began, turning to peer over her shoulder.

"No, don't look." Sir Randall bent forward and took her mouth with his. It was a complete and effective way of silencing her. Larissa had melted with his touch. And with his kiss, she found she was losing her ability for rational thought.

"Really . . ." she gasped, pushing away from him. "You must stop."

"May I remind you, you're the one who dreamed up this little tale. It was all because you didn't want to sleep in a barn. You wanted a warm room and a bed. If you will recall, it was on your behest I played along, not because of any perverted pleasure on my part. Well, madam, this is what has resulted. You have made your bed and I am to lie in it with you."

She knew, of course, he meant figuratively. "Is there nothing we can do to stop this?"

"Nothing I know of. Any ideas you may have on this matter will be more than appreciated. No, no. On second thought, it was your idea that placed us in this predicament. I think it best if *I* think of a way out."

"What are my aunt and your uncle going to say when they return?"

Sir Randall lounged back, resting his arms on the railing. Looking far too comfortable in Larissa's mind. "It would be fair to guess they will wish us the most sincere felicitations."

As soon as the barge docked, she and Sir Randall wasted no time in thanking their host and leaving the premises for Rushton House. When they stepped onto the front walk, Laurie pulled the door open to greet Larissa and Sir Randall. She could feel the weight of public scrutiny lift from her shoulders once she passed through the portal into the safety of the house.

"Shall I instruct Mrs. Drum to bring tea to the parlor?"

"Yes, Laurie, thank you." Sir Randall shed his gloves and handed them to the butler along with his hat.

Larissa observed Sir Randall watch the butler with more than a passing interest. She led the way up the stairs to the first floor and moved on into the parlor.

The ever-efficient Mrs. Drum bustled into the room with her usual vigor. Instead of the endless prattle she usually delivered along with the tea service, she kept silent. Larissa opened her mouth to comment on the oddity, but with the lift of Sir Randall's eyebrows she refrained.

"That's all right, Mrs. Drum, we'll pour." Sir Randall dismissed the housekeeper. She curtsied and took her leave. "The servants know," he whispered.

"What? How can you tell?" Larissa asked.

He made a careful inspection of the doorways and listened for whispers more quiet than their normal hush. "It's what they haven't said," he explained. "It's a minute difference in their behavior, but it's there."

"Really? You would think they, above all, would know. They see how we live," Larissa's voice grew impatient, insistent. "They must know the truth."

"And choose to ignore it."

"Why would they disbelieve what they know is true?" Larissa began to pace.

"Who can say?" Sir Randall settled on the sofa and helped himself to tea. "Would you care for some?" He lifted the pot, offering to pour her a cup.

"How can you sit there and calmly take tea?" she scolded. "Aren't you the least bit concerned?"

"Of course I'm concerned." Sir Randall took on a serious tone. His attention settled to the plate of assorted breads and cakes. "At the moment, what truly concerns me is the lack of apple tarts. They're my favorite." He sorted through the lot, making a thorough search.

"Oh, do stop," she pleaded, feeling the events of the day taking their toll on her already ragged nerves. "Whatever are we to do?"

Sir Randall sat back and lifted his teacup. "Why, finish

our tea. Do have some. I'm sure it will do you a world of good."

"You really are quite impossible," she huffed, disgusted with his attitude and plopped into a chair.

With a "Sir," Laurie announced his presence. "Would you care to peruse the invitations? We seem to have accumulated an unusual abundance this afternoon." He had dispensed with the silver salver and lifted his full hands, producing said invitations.

"Have we?" Sir Randall remarked. Laurie relinquished one handful into Sir Randall's waiting hands and set the second on the table and left. Sir Randall rummaged through the pile in his hand. His eyes widened in surprise.

"I thought everyone understood your uncle would be gone," Larissa said.

"They're not addressed to my uncle, they're addressed to us." Sir Randall handed several to Larissa and rummaged through the others from the table.

Larissa read the first. *Sir Randall and Lady Trent,* it said.

"Vouchers to Almack's," Sir Randall announced with surprise and tapped the parchment with his fingertips. "I've been on the town for the Season before, but never have I flown so high." A burst of laughter escaped from Sir Randall.

"I'm afraid I don't understand."

"We are the latest fashionables." He gave another peal of laughter. "Gad." Sir Randall held up a golden-edged invitation. "This is for the rout at Norfolk House tonight."

"You're not thinking of going are you?"

"Why not? It's Norfolk House. When would we ever

have a chance to attend? It's a great honor. News of our extraordinary marriage, I suppose." A smile crossed Sir Randall's lips. "We have captured the curiosity of the *haute ton*."

"And we shall fall out of favor just as easily, I imagine."

"I have no doubt," he remarked. "Should we not enjoy every fortuitous opportunity that comes our way?"

Larissa said nothing.

"The Duke and Duchess of Norfolk, not to mention the other peers of the kingdom, will be in attendance." Sir Randall went on to tempt her. His eyes glimmered, teasing in the charming way of his. "Don't tell me you aren't the least bit intrigued as to how the better half lives."

Maybe she was . . . just a little.

"The Larissa I knew wanted to live and experience life. We have a chance to do all that and more."

More? Larissa wanted to know what that more might be. "You must already know, your uncle is an earl."

"My uncle, not me. Nor am I fated to inherit that much coveted title." An anxious smile crossed his face. "Laurie, has Mrs. Rutledge arrived yet?"

"No, sir, she has not."

Randall looked back at Larissa. "What do you say? I think we should go."

Larissa tapped the corner of a parchment on her cheek and considered the proposal. After the Season was over, the truth about their marriage would come out. The scandal would force her to live the rest of her life in the country. However, she imagined with the influence of her aunt and new uncle, they could arrange for her to marry quietly. A local squire's son or some other suitable husband could be found. Before she faced that dreary life, she would use to her advantage all that this situation provided.

Sir Randall was right, she'd never have a chance like this again.

"I shall be ready to leave in an hour," she announced.

Chapter Fifteen

Observing the line of carriages waiting to deposit their passengers at Norfolk House, Larissa grew impatient. "Why don't we just walk? It's only a few houses down."

"We can't do that," Sir Randall, who sat in calm reserve against the squabs, answered.

"Why not?" Larissa asked, returning to her seat.

"It's just not done."

"This is preposterous." Larissa peered out the open carriage window again and looked behind them. The long line of carriages stretched down the street and around the corner. "Society people have such odd ways."

When they rounded the corner ten minutes later, Larissa could see the house. The curtains were pulled back, and she saw every window ablaze with light and the crush of people inside.

"Are we to go in there? Faith, I believe there is no room for another soul."

Nearing the head of the line, Larissa saw exiting guests waiting for their carriages to leave. "Look at all these people leaving." Larissa spoke after a lengthy silence. She felt her stomach give an angry grumble. It occurred to her that in her rush to dress, she had forgotten to eat. "I hope we have not missed supper. I'm afraid my stomach would make the most undignified protest."

"Supper?" Sir Randall repeated. "Supper is not served at most routs."

"No supper?" Larissa sighed disappointedly. "Well, I'll just have a few extra cakes to fortify my appetite."

"There is usually no refreshment of any kind served," Sir Randall added. "Nor dancing, nor music for that matter."

Larissa glared at Sir Randall nonplussed. "What kind of party is this? Whatever are we to do here?"

"One attends a rout to see and to be seen, my dear." He smiled and gave her hand a pat. A liveried footman opened the carriage door, leaving Larissa's reaction unspoken.

"I say, this is a fabulous crush," Sir Randall exclaimed after stepping into the townhouse and removing his outer garments.

"Is that good or bad?" Larissa queried, shedding her wrap.

"Good, to be sure." Sir Randall cupped her elbow and led her into the queue on the staircase, moving upward. It seemed to Larissa's dismay their waiting had not ended.

The herd of people shuffled about the staircase, which felt smaller by the minute. Larissa had to endure countless elbows poking her in varying degrees and directions. It occurred to her this was not in the realm of what she considered fun.

Larissa turned to look at the length of the line stretching behind them. It was still all the way out the door with no end in sight.

"Oh!" she cried when thrown against Sir Randall. His hard chest knocked the wind out of her. Sir Randall's hands came up behind her, pressing on her back, holding her to him. Her face was mere inches from his. "Do you mind?" she snapped.

"I do enjoy a successful rout." Larissa heard his words pass through a suggestive smile.

Except he hadn't had the mind to release her. "You did that on purpose," she said through her teeth.

"I most certainly did not," he corrected, pushing her away from him. "Can't be helped really." Sir Randall glanced at the guests compressed around them.

Larissa faced forward, away from Sir Randall, took a few steps forward and saw the first story landing. She allowed her smile to surface. Perhaps he had enjoyed it. Maybe as much as she had.

"Sir Randall and Lady Trent," the liveried footman announced.

On the first story landing, Lady Norfolk greeted her guests. "How nice to see you . . ." her voice trailed. The smile she wore did not, although she did not recognize Sir Randall. She continued in equitable tones, "You are the nephew of the Earl of Rushton, are you not?"

Sir Randall gave a low bow. "Yes, Your Grace."

"How delighted to meet you." The duchess held her hand out to Larissa. "Then you, of course, must be Lady Trent."

Larissa said nothing, accepted the duchess' hand and curtsied. She sensed a newfound interest surge through the duchess.

"I do hope you enjoy my special treat for this evening." Lady Norfolk pulled Larissa closer with her hand. "I have the legendary Briolette diamond on display."

"It is the only such gemstone that could near, but not surpass, your natural beauty, Your Grace," Sir Randall said in an altogether pleasant manner. He smiled, making his already attractive face more handsome. He pulled Larissa's hand from the duchess' grip and tucked it into the crook of his elbow, securing it with his own hand.

"I can see why you had to marry this rascal, Lady Trent. You could not resist him."

"I do continue to try," Larissa replied, forcing a civil smile. By the curious looks surrounding them, the duchess was not the only lady who appeared to envy her and Larissa hated acting the pretense of marriage.

"I shall conduct the viewing from the bust of Zeus in the Great Room."

"We shall be delighted, Your Grace," Sir Randall replied and made a bow before escorting Larissa away.

"You're quite the accomplished flirt," Larissa said.

"That's *very* accomplished flirt," he corrected her.

Larissa hadn't intended the statement to be a compliment.

"You may describe me as a lot of things, but charming must be among them."

"And conceited too, I imagine."

"There is no purpose insulting me. I am merely pointing out what is obvious."

Larissa regarded him with a pointed look. "What is obvious to me is that you need a healthy dose of modesty."

"If it sat on a plate with a fork, I'd have to fight you for it," he retorted in fun.

Beyond the Music Room lay the first of two reception rooms. Larissa carried a glimmer of a hope she might find a morsel to eat and scanned the melee for a circulating servant with a loaded tray in hand.

"If I cannot find at least something to drink, I shall probably faint," Larissa admitted.

Sir Randall sidled up to her, running his hands up her arms and holding her upright. "Then I shall make sure you remain steady."

She tried to wrench out of his hold. "I'd prefer you let me fall to the floor and allow the guests to tread upon me."

"I shan't allow any such thing to happen, my sweet." He bent to whisper in her ear, "Besides, my uncle would have me thrashed within an inch of my life if any harm should befall you."

"Your concern is overwhelming," Larissa remarked. "You may unhand me."

Sir Randall scowled. "I wouldn't hear of it. Can't have you toppling over in the midst of the guests. It would make a most dreadful scene. Things are muddled enough as they are, don't you agree?"

Larissa remained silent, but the stormy expression on her face told him she was not pleased. She needed a diversion to keep her mind off her stomach.

"Look there, the duchess is approaching to lead the group to see her diamond," Sir Randall pointed out.

"If there isn't anything to eat, I suppose we might as well see it," Larissa sighed. She took Sir Randall's arm and fell in line with the others.

Lady Norfolk led five couples upstairs, down the hall, and into a room. Within a glass box the Briolette diamond hung on a sizable gold chain.

The diamond was very large, elongated in shape, about the length of Randall's pinkie finger, and completely faceted.

"The diamond is over ninety carats in size and once belonged to Eleanor of Aquitaine, who acquired it while married to her first husband, Louis VII of France," the Duchess of Norfolk explained. "She gave it to her son, Richard the Lionheart, who used it to pay his release from the Emperor of Austria."

Randall could see the onlookers' heads move from side to side trying to glimpse this sizable chunk of history. He also noticed most of them, at one time or another, staring at him and Larissa, sizing them up as well.

The duchess continued, "It disappeared then resurfaced in the 1500s when Henri II of France presented it to his mistress, Diane de Poitiers. I am proud to say I have recently purchased it and brought it back to England, its original home."

The guests gave a round of polite applause before descending the staircase and returning to the Great Room.

"Not to distract from the *pièce de résistance* of the evening," Randall whispered to Larissa, "but I could not help but notice there was more attention paid to us than to Her Grace of Norfolk's necklace."

If Larissa had been paying more attention to the people

around her instead of to the rumblings of her empty stomach, she might have realized the same. She could see the pointed glances of the guests and nearly hear the waggling of their tongues. The stately posture of a servant in the next room caught her eye, distracting her from the gossiping guests.

"I think I see someone with a tray," she said to Sir Randall. "I'm going to see for myself. Don't leave without me."

"No, I shan't, but you best not go alone," he called to her. It wasn't a moment later when someone came careening into him.

"Excuse me!" Lady Dorothea could probably have avoided bumping into Randall. Her hands moved below the front of his waistband and slowly slid up to their final resting place on his chest. "Such a sad crush, don't you agree?"

With a stern facade and with great care, Randall took hold of her wrists and removed her hands from his person. "Yes, it is."

Dorothea glanced away before blinking her beautiful blue eyes at him. "I would like to apologize for my rude behavior this afternoon."

"You, rude?" Randall gave a gracious, understanding smile. "Not at all. I think you'll find things will have worked for the best."

"You have the right of it, Sir Randall. I have all confidence that things will indeed turn out for the best." Randall saw her smile, which at any other time would have surely bent his will. "If you will excuse me." She squeezed by him and moved toward the doorway.

He was amazed that now he felt very little for her. He had never meant to hurt her. If she had forgiven him, all the better. He would gladly go his way and was relieved to know she would now go hers.

"Do my eyes deceive me? Is that you, Randall?" Randall did an about-face and spotted Lord William Felgate shouldering through the crowd, heading in his direction. "How goes it, old man?"

"Wills, it's been an age since I've seen you." It did Randall good to see a friendly, familiar face. "Are you going by Lord Felgate yet?"

"No. And don't think I ever will. Terrance is attending the Season looking for a wife. Plans to set up a nursery."

"Ah, so you're about to be bumped down to presumptive heir," Randall clarified.

"Speaking of wives. Heard you've taken the fatal step." William gave a wry smile. "Where is your charming bride?" He stood up on tiptoe, looking around the sea of guests, trying to spot the girl that could catch Randall's fancy.

"I was wrong," Larissa sighed, returning to Sir Randall's side.

"This is she, I presume. Why would you want to keep her hidden away?" William took Larissa's hand and brought it to his lips. "Charmed, my lady."

"Allow me," Randall offered. "My dear, this is Lord William Felgate. Lord William, here, is my good friend."

"*Very* good," William stressed, keeping an appreciative eye on Larissa.

Randall glanced at Larissa before confessing, "We're not really married, Wills."

"Why would you deny it?" William said in disbelief. "She's everything you'd ever want!"

"You see," Randall said to Larissa. "Even he doesn't believe me."

The success of the rout was overoccupied, overstated, and overblown in Larissa's estimation. She found it very hard to believe people actually wanted to attend these dreadful affairs. With nothing to eat or drink, no music or entertainment, she didn't see the value of attending.

Now that it was over and done with, she and Sir Randall could return to the comfort of Rushton house and its ready and well-stocked kitchen. They descended the stairs, retrieved their outerwear and, after waiting another lifetime, stood at the curb next in line for the return of their carriage.

A steady murmur of voices increased with intensity as a group moved from the house toward the street. "What's going on?" she whispered to Sir Randall.

"I'm not quite sure," he answered. "But we'll soon find out."

Sure enough, Lady Goddard, who stood just behind them, said to Mrs. Witharm, "I can't possibly imagine. With a house full of people?"

"*I* think it must have been one of the guests," Mrs. Witharm replied.

"No, it cannot be true. One of the duchess' friends?"

Mrs. Witharm looked down her nose at the other guests in line. "Not everyone in attendance is a friend of Her Grace."

Feeling self-conscious, Larissa faced forward, knowing Mrs. Witharm had meant someone of a lower class. Someone like her, a mere niece of a dowager viscountess or the wife of a baronet.

"The terrace window was left open," Lady Goddard continued, relaying the facts. "They say that is how the thief escaped."

"From two floors above ground? I think not, unless he was an acrobat from Astley's."

The Rushton coach pulled up next. A footman opened the door and handed Larissa up. She pulled her skirts around her legs, settling in the seat. Across from her sat Sir Randall. He nodded to the footman who signaled to the driver to move the carriage off.

"Did you hear those ladies?" she asked Sir Randall. "Do you have any idea what was stolen?" Larissa felt alarm that one of the guests, perhaps even someone they knew, might be the guilty party.

Sir Randall leaned back against the squabs and slid his hands into his pockets to reflect on the matter. Then he coolly replied, "I need not wonder what it was or who has it. I know." With that he pulled a thick-braided gold chain from his pocket. Hanging from the chain hung the Briolette diamond.

Chapter Sixteen

Larissa gasped in shock and pointed. "How . . . how . . . how . . ."

"They'll think *I've* pinched the bloody thing."

"Well, *they* just might be right," Larissa said and gazed at him, wide-eyed. "Did you?"

"Of course not. However, the same who believe we're married will just as easily accept the notion I took this." Sir Randall cast an accusing glance in Larissa's direction. "I do believe there is one of us that has been known to stray from the path of truth every now and again."

"Are you accusing *me* of lying?" she retorted.

"I need not imply. I know it for a fact. You forget, I spent some time as your husband, *Mr. Quinn.*"

"How is it you come to have the necklace?" She glanced at the diamond pendant in Sir Randall's hand.

"I'm not entirely sure, but with all the jostling and

shoving that goes on at a rout, someone could have easily slid it into my pocket without my knowledge."

"But who would have done such a terrible thing?"

"I'm not entirely sure. But I need to return it. Anonymously of course."

"Of course," she agreed. "And just how do you plan to accomplish this?"

"I'm not quite sure," he said. The coach came to a stop in front of Rushton house. "But I will think of something." He slid the jewel back into his pocket.

The following afternoon, Larissa walked into the so-called blue parlor. She had not meant to surprise Sir Randall, but found him leaning over the table. It almost looked as if he were concealing something.

"Oh, it's you." Sir Randall lurched, spinning to face Larissa when he heard her enter.

"What have you there?" Larissa peered to see what he had behind his back.

"It's . . ." Sir Randall glanced around in the empty room. "The necklace," he whispered.

Larissa mimicked him and looked about before speaking. "You still have it?"

"When would I have had an opportunity to rid myself of it?"

"I'm sure I don't know," she said, indignant.

"I can't just hand the thing over to one of the footmen and have him leg it to the duchess with my profound apologies, now, can I?" He slid the small package into his pocket.

"I suppose not. How do you plan to . . ."

"Please—" He shushed her. "Not so loud."

"As you can see for yourself, Sir Randall, we are quite alone."

"One cannot be too careful." His dark eyes, marked with a tinge of suspicion, stared into hers. "As they say, the walls have ears."

"Do they?" Larissa widened her eyes, mimicking his, and looked around the room.

"How do you think the servants know so much?"

Larissa imagined an eye watching at every crack and an ear pressed at every door. Heeding the warning, she slid closer and spoke in a hushed voice. "What *are* you planning?"

"Well," he began. "I am planning to return this to Norfolk House by post."

"By post?"

"The duchess will gladly pay the post for its return, and I will be equally glad to be rid of it. They'd have the devil of a time tracing it back to me." He shrugged at the simplicity of his idea. "Nothing will look amiss. We'll look to all the world to be an ordinary couple, out about the streets attending to everyday errands."

"We?" Larissa repeated in alarm.

"With your help I'm sure I could manage."

"My help? I don't want you to make me a part of this."

Sir Randall smiled. "You're already a part of this, involved beyond belief."

"No," she groaned in denial. But it was true. She hadn't thought of it, but her alliance with him, however imagined, was real in the minds outside that room. It was a premise she had hardly had a chance to warm up to. Everyone else thought she and Sir Randall were married. Everyone. She had to remember that. If she could be of help to him, she should cooperate.

"All right," she agreed against her better judgment. "I'll accompany you."

"Thank you." He smiled.

When Larissa and Randall returned from running their morning errands, including a successful trip to the post office, the butler informed them, "While you were out, a Mrs. Rutledge stopped by."

"My aunt's companion," Larissa reminded Randall as they exchanged looks.

He recalled exactly who Mrs. Rutledge was, he had just forgotten about the chaperone's due arrival. "Where is she now, Laurie? And what the devil's kept her? She was supposed to be here yesterday."

"I did not inquire, sir. It seems in light of recent events, Mrs. Rutledge thought it best to use her time in London to better advantage by visiting her sister before returning home and awaiting further word from the countess."

"She left? Returning home?" Larissa did not sound pleased. "What are we—"

"How did she come to learn these 'recent events?'" Randall asked, suspicious that the butler might have been the source of the news.

"I cannot say, sir," Laurie replied with his indomitably impassive face. "And there is a Lord William Felgate waiting to see you."

Lord William waited in the parlor and stood when Larissa and Randall entered the room. "I hate to pop in unexpectedly on you like this." William shrugged his shoulders apologetically.

"What a pleasant surprise, Wills. Do sit down."

Mrs. Drum brought the tea cart. Larissa waved her away, poured, and handed the first cup to their guest.

"Bumping into you last night reminded me it's been at least a year since I've seen you." Lord William accepted his tea. "I'll be dashing off to the old fortress in a few days. Had enough of the social scene, if you know what I mean. Would you care to join me?"

Larissa remained quiet and watched several emotions play over Sir Randall's face.

"Oh, do say you'll come," Lord William urged, sounding near desperation. "It's going to be ghastly dull about the old place without you."

"Me?" Sir Randall gulped.

"And your lovely wife, of course," Lord William added, bestowing upon Larissa a magnetic smile.

"Yes, why not," Sir Randall agreed. Larissa rested her disbelieving stare on him.

What was the man thinking?

"It's all settled then." Lord William placed his untouched tea on the low table and shot to his feet. "Thanks for the tea," he said while making for the door.

"You haven't touched yours yet," Larissa called after him.

"Must be off," he said. "I've still Terrance to tell of our company." She could hear Lord William's staccato steps dancing down the stairs.

"I do believe your wits have gone begging." Larissa glared at Sir Randall, mystified at his effrontery.

"I think it really might be best if we disappeared into the country. Let this matter of the marriage scandal cool."

That was enough for her. In the country, she would be safe. Away from London, away from the gossip, she need not endure the torturous advances Sir Randall made toward her for the *ton's* benefit. Unfortunately, she would not be away from him. And the one person she felt she needed the most protection from was Sir Randall.

That afternoon, William's coach waited outside for Larissa's and Sir Randall's luggage.

"We'll be traveling in Lord William's transport with him. Please make sure the trunks are loaded and sent with Abby," Sir Randall instructed Laurie.

"As you say, sir."

Sir Randall glared at Larissa. "I'll not have you telling anyone like Mrs. Briggs your husband considers you not genteel enough to have a lady's maid this time."

With a final farewell to Laurie and without the presence of Mrs. Rutledge, Larissa, Sir Randall, and Lord William departed for Carswell Castle. Just four hours outside London, Larissa knew the trip would be a short one.

Lord William had already succumbed to the transport's motion. Reclining against the far corner with his feet propped up on the seat, he was fast asleep. Sir Randall sat across from her.

"I've left word with Laurie where we can be reached and instructions that it is imperative Uncle Cyrus should do so when he returns. I have no doubt he'll soon have everything all right and tight. You'll see," Sir Randall assured Larissa. He removed his hat and tossed it in the seat next to her.

"And until then, do Lord Melton and Lord William expect to see us as a married couple?" Larissa wondered if Sir Randall's forward ways would indeed be left in London.

"As gentlemen, men anyway, I do not believe they would ever notice the difference." Sir Randall leaned across the coach and murmured, "Unless of course, you *wish* me to continue to dote on you as a loving husband?"

"I *wish* you would stay in your own seat, if you please," she remarked, pushing him back.

Sir Randall laughed. "My dear, you have the most charming ways about you."

Larissa glanced at the dozing Lord William. "I would hate to assume he couldn't hear us. Is that not what placed us in this bumblebroth to start?"

"He'll not be hearing anything I haven't told him already. It's not my fault he doesn't believe we're not man and wife. I promise, Larissa, while we are married I shall behave as a proper husband should. I would not for the world make you look like a fool by parading with another woman behind your back."

"By 'proper husband' you mean . . ."

"All I meant was proper escort, companion, until such time you no longer need my protection."

"Of course. I could not have any objection to that."

"It is to assure you are properly looked after, I'm afraid your aunt would insist."

"As would your uncle."

"And how right he would be," Sir Randall confirmed with every confidence.

One of the coach's wheels hit a rut in the road. Lord

William sprang awake. "I do beg you pardon," he murmured, a hint of sleep remained in his voice, giving it a rasp. "Must have dropped off." He pushed his hat back onto his forehead and drew a hand over his eyes. "Have I missed anything?"

Atop the rise in the distance stood Carswell Castle. "There it is," Lord William announced several hours later. The coach headed up the long drive.

"I can see you're disappointed in the old place. It has a moat, battlements, and towering turrets looming from above," Lord William enlightened her. "Everything one could want in a castle. My brother knows all the who-built-what-when. He can tell you names and dates if you are really interested. I'm not. It's a crumbly old thing. Ghastly, really."

Stepping into the main house, William announced, "Here we are."

"Shall I have tea served?" Jenkins asked, taking the travelers' outerwear.

"Tea? Deuced hot and dusty ride we've been on." William offered with distaste, appearing to forget his guests. "Oh, yes, by all means, tea . . . in the parlor."

Larissa and Randall followed William down the hall until he came to a stop, reluctant to step into the parlor where refreshments were to be served. William eyed the doorway across the hall. Behind closed door lay a gentleman's domain. A safe haven, a fine collection of books, and most importantly, a well-stocked supply of liquor.

"Would you care to take a turn about the garden before

we sit to take tea?" Randall asked Larissa. "I know I could do with stretching my legs a bit."

"Sounds like a splendid idea," she replied, accepting Randall's outstretched arm.

"Care to join us?" he asked, glancing up at William, who grew nervous with anticipation.

"No, no, you go right on ahead." His answer was quick. "You must see the rose arbor. It's toward the back, on the far left side of the garden. New since you've been here last," William directed at Randall. "No need to hurry, though. Do take your time," he said while waving them out the back door.

Randall could not hide his amusement at his friend's eagerness to drive them away so he could smuggle into the library for a spot of drink. He knew William didn't consider tea worth the water it was made with.

When he and Larissa stepped into the garden, she pulled her hand from Randall's arm, and kept a steady pace beside him. "I think I could learn to like this," she said, taking in the expansive surroundings.

"It is very nice," Randall replied. Not only did he admire the well-maintained gardens, but it was Larissa he viewed as he spoke.

"There's the rose garden." She pointed and jogged ahead, disappearing through the volume of flowering bushes. They grew in profusion along the latticed sides of the wide arbor.

Randall leaned against a pole and watched her stroll along the lined rosebushes on the far side of the enclosed garden. She admired the flowers on each bush and sampled the fragrance of only a few as she passed. Completing her tour, she stopped under the arch, refusing to near him.

He felt a slow, lazy smile steal across his lips. "Shall I tell you the bloom on your cheek exactly matches the blush of that rose?"

Her eyes shifted to gaze at the pink of the flower, then lowered, glancing to the ground. "I've done it now," he chided himself. "I've put you to the blush, throwing the similarity off. You're nearly crimson."

He reached out and touched her, tilting her chin up. His fingers savored the smoothness of her skin. Randall felt intoxicated with the warm scent of roses surrounding him.

Larissa drew a long, slow breath, and whispered, "You promised." No doubt she read his thought.

He removed his hand. "So I did" was his woeful reply. "In the future, I must remember not to make such pronouncements in haste. I've already come to regret this one."

After their stroll, Larissa and Sir Randall sat down to tea. Lord William did join them, but did not drink.

"I've instructed Jenkins to place you on the first floor of the west wing with me," Lord William explained. "The old place is rather large. If we don't share the same floor we might not see each other for days."

Larissa finished her tea and set aside her cup. After tea, she and Sir Randall were shown to their rooms.

Because of the twelve-foot-high ceilings, huge tapestries were draped throughout the house. Larissa was shown to her room first. Once inside, she threw the bolt on the door and eased onto the bed.

Peace, quiet, and solitude. How pleasant this all was, how easily she could accept these surroundings.

"Very nice," Sir Randall drawled, appearing by the side of the bed unannounced and totally unexpected. "And I see we have the place all to ourselves."

"How did you get in here?" she demanded, pulling herself into a sitting position.

"Through the connecting door," he replied, smiling as if he were the proverbial cat in the cream pot.

Chapter Seventeen

"Connecting door? What connecting door?" Larissa demanded.

"The connecting door between our rooms." He made a gesture over his shoulder to indicate the direction.

Larissa climbed off the bed and followed him at a respectable distance to the opened dressing room doors. "Where is it?"

"Right here," he announced, gesturing to the gaping portal.

She inched closer, but did not move into his room. "That's your room in there?" Larissa gazed into the masculine domain.

"Yes." Randall stepped past her, into his room. "Would you care to inspect the habitat of the mysterious male of the species?"

"N-no," she stuttered. Her gaze crept beyond him and conducted a silent inspection. Offering to share a room with him was the worst thing she had ever done. She should have slept in the barn.

Larissa slammed the door closed in his face and bolted it. That would put an end to his unwanted visitations. And hopefully keep her curiosity on her side of the door.

At the breakfast table the next morning, Larissa did her best to ignore Sir Randall. She sipped at her hot chocolate and nibbled at her buttered toast with just the smallest dab of preserves. Randall enjoyed a cup of coffee with his plateful of eggs, ham, and sausage.

William, who had forgone his meal, had a cup of coffee at his elbow. "Look here, Randall, you've made the paper." William folded the *Morning Post* and held it upright for closer inspection, " 'Since the recent discovery of the marriage of Sir R— and Lady T—,it seems they are not the only members of their family to enter into blissful union. The Earl of R— and Lady C— have followed their younger relatives to the altar.' Now what do you think of that?"

"Not much really. You know gossip." Randall shrugged and paid more attention to Larissa, who ignored the both of them and excused herself, pushing away from the table.

Randall wanted to rid himself of further discussion about his uncle, Larissa's aunt, and his own marriage altogether. He needed to patch the rift he had created the day before. He dabbed his mouth with the linen napkin, set it aside and followed Larissa out the door.

It didn't take him long to find her. She had settled in the sunny parlor working on some type of sewing. Randall strolled in and circled around to see the face of her hoop.

"What are you working on there?" he asked. She glanced up at him. It did not appear he was a welcome sight.

"A panel I started when I first arrived in London. I have not had a chance to work on it since. I must admit I value my quiet. I find this a refreshing change from the last few months."

"Do you?" He studied her face for a trace of encouragement. He didn't know if she would allow him to stay. "They're always in need of company of some kind to fill their house," Randall said, venturing on a new topic. "I've been coming here for years. Wills manages to have me stay at least three or four weeks at a time. The place is so monstrously large, I haven't been in half the rooms myself." Randall settled into an overstuffed chair.

"I have noticed many doors are closed," she said, flowing into an easy conversation.

"Who knows what torture chambers lie behind those doors?" he teased her.

Her eyes widened in shock and she gave a little gasp. "Really?" She displayed an ever so charming look of complete gullibility.

Randall leaned forward. "Don't be a goose. The torture chambers are in the dungeon below ground."

Larissa narrowed her eyes and gave Sir Randall a guarded look. He was just roasting her.

"Wills and his brother are the only occupants. As you probably have noticed, most of the house is shut up."

"I had wondered," she admitted. Her fingers continued to work the needle.

"It's all right to have a look around if you want." His

tone made it sound almost like a challenge. She glanced at him to discern his meaning.

"Thank you, I think I just might." Despite the subtle warning, Larissa planned to explore the lower level of the great house.

What she had expected was for the men, Sir Randall and Lord William, to be off doing whatever it was men did in the country, while she could be left to her own devices.

Her own devices would be no more than needlework, reading, and walks in the garden. Perhaps if she grew adventurous she'd wander outside the castle walls for an extended outing. Since she didn't ride, she couldn't stray far.

What she hadn't planned on was Sir Randall's constant company. It all came about so gradually. That evening he joined her in the drawing room after supper. She closed her book and they passed the hours in comfortable conversation.

The following evening, they took turns reading aloud. He acted out every line. How she had enjoyed that!

The next day, he happened by her in the garden and accompanied her for the remainder of her stroll. How she could enjoy his company, and how he could make her laugh! This routine set the pattern for the several days that followed.

That afternoon at tea, the look he gave her was so . . . so . . . intimate. He spoke very little at tea, only an occasional please or thank you, but he was far from silent. It was his eyes. When their gazes met, she could feel the flush of warmth wash into her cheeks.

When she handed him his second cup, his fingers brushed against her hand, sending a shiver up her arm.

Sir Randall smiled. He knew exactly what he was doing to her. He might have done it on purpose. From his previous behavior, she had just cause to be suspicious. Riveted on the fingers that had brushed so casually against hers, she watched him grip the handle of his cup and followed the cup to his mouth.

It was the beginning of her undoing.

That mouth. His mouth. And those lips moved into an enchanting smile. She watched with rapt attention as they pursed to blow upon his tea. When he tipped the cup to drink, Larissa gasped when the cup intervened, depriving her of the sight of his magnificent mouth. How she ached for those lips, to see them, to watch them, to feel them. Larissa knew she had to feel them on hers once again.

It was later that day when Larissa noticed that one of the doors, which had previously been closed, was now open. She approached with caution, pushing the door only wide enough to peer in.

What lay behind the door was concealed in darkness, until the drapes were thrown open by a maid, sending motes of dust flying in every direction.

"Am I allowed in?" Larissa asked, still hovering outside the door.

"Yes, my lady. I've been ordered to air out the room for his lordship's return." The maid bobbed a curtsy and continued with her work.

Larissa entered the room. A pianoforte stood in the far corner. The fireplace lay on the right. The wall opposite held built-in bookshelves, drawers, and glass display cases.

She perused the many books on the shelves and examined the items in the glass cases. Inside, various small hand instruments, different types of flutes, and a wide variety of stringed instruments were displayed.

Embarrassed to sit at the pianoforte with an audience, Larissa strolled up and down the room to study its contents until the maid finished her dusting.

During this idle time, it occurred to Larissa the point of coming to the country was for her and Sir Randall to keep their distance from one another. And they were doing anything but.

That morning after breakfast, Sir Randall had taken care to introduce the occupants of the stables. She had always been afraid of horses. Her fear stemmed from her unfamiliarity. With Sir Randall acquainting her with every horse safely behind their stable door, Larissa discovered each had a personality. By the end of the tour, she had her own favorites: the bay mare, Hera, and the dappled gray, Achilles.

Sir Randall told her learning to ride was a simple matter and she had begun to believe him. It occurred to her if he could convince her to overcome her fear of horses, what else could he talk her into?

For all intents and purposes, her reputation in London could be considered ruined, but she still had her pride.

What was she to make of his constant company? Why was he spending so much time with her? It didn't help that she experienced her own confusion when it came to him. She longed for him when he was absent and dreaded his nearness when he was present. Being near him was growing more and more difficult to tolerate. Sometimes the desire to touch him, to have him hold her and kiss her was so overwhelming she wanted to scream.

Larissa sat at the keyboard of the pianoforte and confirmed the instrument was in tune. She paged through the sheet music already displayed and found nothing of interest. She decided to play a Mozart piece from memory. Unfocused thoughts of Sir Randall came to mind and a smile spread across her lips.

It was no wonder she had fallen in love with him.

Her hands froze, poised above the keys. The smile on her lips faded. *Fallen in love?* Had she actually thought those words to herself?

Larissa tried to recall where she had left off and she resumed the piece.

She *was* in love with him. She knew it, she could feel it in her soul and in the recesses of her heart . . . in love.

Following the delightful music emanating from the music room, Randall stopped just inside the door and admired the artist. Larissa sat at the keyboard, staring in his direction, but oblivious to his presence.

He didn't know she could play. Actually, when he thought about it, there wasn't much he really knew about her at all. During their walks the past few days, they never spoke of personal things.

Larissa looked lovely and serene, unaware she was being watched. It was the ever so slight tilt of her head, the way her eyes moved when she glanced down at her hands.

"That was beautiful," he said. Larissa looked up and watched Randall walk into the room toward the pianoforte. "I did not know you knew how to play."

"There are many details you do not know about me."

"It is not due to lack of interest, I can assure you."

She flipped through the pages of the sheet music and must have felt his stare for an attractive blush crept across her cheeks.

He settled onto the bench beside her. "I had no idea you were so talented." He smiled. Randall recognized the sensual quality in his voice. He had promised to behave himself, but she made it so deucedly difficult.

Sitting mere inches away, the impulse to stroke her soft cheek, cup her chin and tilt her face to his almost overtook him. He wanted more than anything to slide her across the polished wood bench toward him, trap her within his arms.

Chapter Eighteen

Randall's head had cleared of the confusion that plagued him that afternoon. When the dinner gong sounded, he hurried to the drawing room and waited. Waited for her. Pacing in front of the sofa, he alternated steps with the wringing of his hands.

Imagine, *he* was nervous. Nervous over a female, no less. If it hadn't been so true the situation might have been laughable. Settling on to the sofa and crossing his legs, he clamped his hand onto his shin to keep his leg from swinging with impatience.

Larissa arrived with a sound of fabric rustling in the doorway. She was dressed in a simple, palest-of-pink gown, and her hair was piled on top of her head with a tantalizing tendril curling down her lovely, soft neck that he would have dearly loved, at that very moment, to nuzzle.

"Evening." Randall nearly fell, forgetting to uncross his legs before shooting to his feet.

"Sir Randall," she returned just above a whisper and smiled at him.

It would not have surprised him if his mouth were gaping open, for he was reduced to a love-struck school boy. What was happening to him?

Randall wanted her to stand there so he could enjoy her loveliness forever, but he knew that was impossible. Afraid to kiss her hand, he paused, inhaling the mild scent of roses he associated with her.

Larissa's lips parted and she gave a barely audible gasp when his lips brushed against the back of her hand. He lingered for a moment, savoring the soft feel and fragrant scent of her skin.

What should he say? What should he do? Randall was spared any decisions when William came striding into the room, breaking their private exchange.

"Letter from Terrance." William waved the missive about for all to see. "He'll be joining us by the end of the week. Says he's invited one of the *ton*'s lovely ladies."

"Does he say which?" Randall asked, not really all that anxious to know. With Larissa's hand still in his, he rubbed her palm with his thumb, dreading to surrender his hold.

"No, but I imagine she must be someone quite exceptional."

"No doubt." Randall shrugged. It really was no concern of his.

"And look here," William went on. "Remember the do at Norfolk's? That enormous diamond necklace the duchess had on display, the one that was stolen? The one belonging to Queen Catherine the Great, or some other historical monarch."

"That's Eleanor of Aquitaine," Randall corrected. "And yes, I remember. How could we ever forget? It was the talk of the town when we left."

"Terrance says it's been returned."

"Really?" Randall glanced to Larissa who gave what he interpreted to be a look of relief.

"Doesn't say who pinched the thing though, but its return was a bit on the unusual side."

"How's that?" Randall prompted.

William drew his finger down the parchment, reading the text. "Says it came by post."

"That *is* odd." Randall exchanged a weighted glance with Larissa, who had the good form not to respond.

"The investigation is called off due to a lack of evidence. Much to the dismay of her grace." William chucked. "She wants 'heads to roll' over this. The duchess was always one for drama, wasn't she?"

Jenkins, the butler, appeared at the door and announced that dinner was served.

Supper tonight lacked all conversation. The meaningful glances that passed between Randall and Larissa apparently went unnoticed by William, who kept a running monologue from the consommé to the fruit and nuts served for dessert.

Instead of retiring to the drawing room, Larissa crossed the garden to the old castle wall. She strolled the sentry walk in search of a cool place to escape the abnormally warm evening.

A breeze ruffled the treetops and drifted across the crenellated battlements. A three-quarter moon lit the four-century-old walkway. The stars twinkled against the black velvet sky. Looking down the winding road that led to the castle, she tried to imagine what it was like to see a knight stampeding toward the drawbridge after a triumphant slaying of a nearby dragon.

"I can see you as a lady in distress." It was Sir Randall.

His arrival did not surprise her. "I did not realize I needed saving."

He inched closer with every word. "Didn't you know?"

"Who, pray tell, should save me?"

"I had imagined myself to be the knight in shining armor."

"I had imagined you as the fire-breathing dragon." She covered her mouth to keep from laughing too hard or too loud.

"And you, dear damsel, have single-handedly struck the mortal blow." He struck his chest with a fist and stumbled to the side.

"I didn't know you wanted to be an actor."

Sir Randall's recovery was instantaneous. "You know, I've always believed I had a natural ability," he said in a tone that lacked all modesty.

"It would not take much to convince me. Aside from my brief London stay this summer, the only acting I am familiar with is the amateur plays done at the Seminary by the girls." She realized how unworldly she must have sounded. "My experience is limited." The instant the words passed her lips she knew it was a mistake.

By the minute change in Sir Randall's stance and the softening of his voice, she sensed he noticed her unintentional double entendre.

"One can learn to appreciate what one doesn't understand."

Larissa's breath caught for a moment. Was he thinking the same thing she was? Did he want the same thing she did? The warm scent of Sir Randall's skin mingled with the cool breeze. Larissa said nothing, but placed her hand lightly upon his chest.

Randall moved closer and brushed his fingertips over her cheek. He drew her face toward his and his warm lips pressed against hers, covering her mouth. They moved with a slow deliberateness that melted her insides. Excitement coiled inside her in a place where her resolve, her willpower once dwelt. She feared now it had deserted her.

His kiss was as she remembered. No, it was much, much better. Tentativeness replaced determination, leisure replaced haste, sweetness replaced any trace of false affection.

And it seemed the most natural thing in the world. Randall decided he would gladly accept the reprimand once the deed was done. But longing, necessity, and instinct dictated that he act. He waited no longer.

When their lips parted, she gasped for air. He covered her open mouth with his, deepening their kiss. Randall pulled away and trailed kisses from her face to her neck and showed no signs of slowing his progress downward. His hands move up and down the length of her back, then slid to her waist.

"Do you mind if I join you?"

"William!" Neither shock nor surprise was the word to describe Randall's response. He fairly pushed Larissa away and braced himself against the wall. William came striding forward.

Where the devil had he come from? Randall wondered.

"Not at all," Randall replied. He closed his eyes and pushed an unsteady hand though his hair, taking slow, deep, even breaths. "We were just looking for a place to find a cool breeze." There was one consolation. Larissa looked just as disturbed as he felt.

"Ghastly weather." William swept a hand over his forehead. "I beg your pardon," he said, loosening his cravat. "I must have this wretched thing off this instant. Can't remember when it's been so blasted hot." He hopped up to sit on the battlement and stared in the distance before starting his monologue.

Randall heard William drone on and lost the thread of his conversation completely. He could see Larissa paid no more attention to William than he. Larissa arched her neck and gazed at him out of the corner of her eye. She returned his stare with an openness that he would have found quite shocking coming from anyone else.

At this moment, she looked so very beautiful. The simple, desolate setting of the walk, the twinkling background of the stars, somehow knowing her affection equaled his. What did he think he was doing? He was driving himself mad with those kinds of thoughts.

The following afternoon, just before she entered the library, Larissa glimpsed Lord William and Sir Randall at the foot of the stairs. Lord William had not seen her.

However, Sir Randall caught sight of her in that precious instant and bestowed upon her the most intimate of smiles, meant for her alone, filled with warmth, longing, and promise. She could feel her heart pound a little stronger. In the privacy of the library she spun with her arms outstretched.

Life was wonderful! To be in love was wonderful! Sir Randall was wonderful!

She replaced the book she had borrowed and removed 'Volume Two.' How long would it be before she would see him again? Perhaps he would not wait until tea. Perhaps he would change his clothes and come down to the library straight away, knowing she waited within.

Larissa heard a voice. Was it Sir Randall? She listened more carefully. Lord William?

"Good to be home again."

It was Lord William's brother, the Marquess of Melton.

Then she heard a female voice. No, two, but much too soft to make out words.

Curiosity got the better of her and she inched out of the library, gaining speed down the hall only to find herself standing face-to-face with Lady Dorothea Brookhurst.

Chapter Nineteen

The next thing Larissa knew she was running upstairs. She stopped in front of Sir Randall's room. She thought better of standing in the hall to knock and made straight for her own room to the doors that joined to his accommodations. She unbolted the lock and rapped upon the door.

The door opened, revealing Sir Randall with a wound, untied cravat, trailing from his neck.

"I'm surprised to see you take advantage of this entry," he said amused. "How nice to see you." Larissa followed him when he moved back to his glass to continue his task, taking up the trailing linen.

"Lord Melton has returned."

"Has he?" Sir Randall murmured without much interest and continued to work on his cravat. With a few finishing touches, he held the linen to make a final tug and twist here and there, adjusting the sides.

"And Lady Dorothea is with him."

165

At the suddenness of the news, Sir Randall's hand pulled much too hard, unraveling the intricate pattern, causing the linen to once again hang free.

"Did you hear what I said? Lady Dorothea is here." Larissa stared at the blank expression on his face.

"It is of no import," he responded, fingering his limp linen. "This one's ruined." He wrenched it from his neck and retrieved another from the clothespress and began again.

She stared at Sir Randall, not at his deft, moving fingers. What puzzled her was his lack of interest in Lady Dorothea. Larissa's words came out with great difficulty, but she had to know. "Are you and she not . . ."

"Yes," Sir Randall answered in a firm tone. His gaze never wavering from his reflection in the glass. "She and I are *not*."

"What if she causes problems? The two of you were at one time close."

"What has transpired between Dorothea and me was over before *our* relationship was revealed. I am certain she is not here to make my acquaintance." Randall gave a tug here and a pull there, the cravat held its shape. "She probably doesn't know we are here. It's all pure speculation on our part. I suggest you ignore her and carry on. If she's on a different floor or in another wing, we need not see her the entire length of our stay."

Larissa imagined it might be possible, but something told her it was highly improbable.

"We meet again, Lady Trent." Lady Dorothea and her mother entered the drawing room for tea. "I trust you will not run away this time."

"I apologize for my behavior earlier. Your presence surprised me and . . ."

Dorothea shook her head. "Please, there is no need to explain. Our situation may be considered unusual, at best. I am certain we will see our way through."

"Yes, it is. And we shall," Larissa answered, growing confident but still apprehensive of Lady Dorothea's manner.

"You left before the Season was over," Lady Brookhurst went on while she poured from the teapot. "You missed the Fortescue rout and the Lady Shelby's ball. That's where Dorothea met Melton."

It was obvious to Larissa that Dorothea's mother was more than pleased with the match. While Dorothea showed no response at the mention of her admirer's name.

"Well, I must admit I was feeling a bit out of sorts after the news about you and Sir Randall," Dorothea confessed. "After meeting Melton, I can honestly say it was all for the best."

"Really?"

"Oh, yes," Dorothea replied and smiled a whimsical smile, raising the cup to her lips. This convinced Larissa there was a possibility of tender feelings in her quarter. "He's a marquess, you know. Very handsome, charming, *and* very rich. How could I not be enchanted with him?"

Was that not similar to what Larissa had told herself about Lord Fenton?

"We are to stay in the same house. I hope we will become fast friends. I do not see for the world why not."

"I suppose you're right. There are only the three of us ladies about," Larissa said.

"That's right, and we shall become very close after a week or two."

"Why, yes," Larissa agreed, finally accepting Dorothea's explanation. "I can see that we might at that." She picked up her hoop and found her needle.

"What are you working on?" Dorothea asked.

"Just a bit of embroidery."

"How lovely it is." Dorothea lifted the edge to admire the pattern. "What are you planning to do with it?"

"Frame it, or perhaps make a pillow. I've not yet decided."

"It would make a lovely cushion, I should think."

Larissa held it at arm's length, imagining it as such. "Perhaps you are right."

"The men have gone coursing," Dorothea announced. She retired her porcelain set onto the tray and remained standing. By her manner it appeared she did not intend to remain. "It seems we ladies are to fend for ourselves."

"Why couldn't they have brought us along?" Larissa complained. Beside the fact that she could not ride, it was the principal of the thing.

"Well, dear, if you are in a delicate condition, you shouldn't be riding at all," Lady Brookhurst was quick in answering, giving Larissa a quick glance at her midsection.

"Maman, please," Dorothea scolded. "Do not listen to her, Lady Trent. You shall see, we ladies shall make due."

"Well, I'm on my way to see Lady Iversly," Lady Brookhurst excused herself.

"Maman, you cannot go alone," Dorothea complained.

"Fustian, my dear, I shall have Regina ride along with me and you two have each other for company."

Later that afternoon, Dorothea entered the music room just as Larissa finished playing. "You play very well," she complimented. "I do not believe I have heard anything finer in any London parlor."

"You are very kind to say so. Do you play?"

"Yes, not the pianoforte, but the violin. It should prove quite diverting to play together while we share this vast, empty house, don't you think?"

"You and I? Playing duets . . . together?" Larissa reflected.

"Duets are usually comprised of two playing together." The smile on Dorothea's face denoted the remark was made in jest, and with not a hint of malice. "Pity I have not an instrument at my disposal."

"But there is a violin." Larissa rose and moved into the far, darkened corner of the room. Opening the glass doors, she took the violin and bow from its case and handed it to Dorothea.

Dorothea plucked the strings to determine the pitch then tightened the strings on the instrument. With Larissa at the keyboard to play the appropriate notes, Dorothea had soon tuned the violin and was ready to play.

After tightening the bow, Dorothea played the scales, limbering her fingers, showing amazing dexterity. The notes resonated clear and strong—she could indeed play well.

"Is there a suitable piece?" Dorothea asked.

"There are several drawers filled with music. I should

be very surprised if we could not find one to both our liking," Larissa replied.

Side by side, they rummaged through the sheaves of sheet music and found several that would do nicely. After choosing an agreed upon appropriate selection, Larissa and Dorothea practiced during the remaining hours of the afternoon.

The next morning, Randall managed a few minutes alone with Larissa at the breakfast table. The afternoon walks and shared evenings they had enjoyed had dwindled away with Dorothea's arrival. His discomfort with her presence did not compare to that of her newfound friendship with Larissa.

"Don't you find it odd?" he asked Larissa.

"I thought as much at first, but as of late, I am under the opinion she is only being friendly. She is ever so nice to me."

"I would advise you to watch yourself."

She gave him a hard stare. "I believe you're envious of our association."

He choked on his coffee. "I beg your pardon? Nothing could be further from the truth." Randall had resented Dorothea's interference. He and Larissa had spent such a glorious time together before the other guests arrived.

But he wasn't as selfish as all that. He was only speaking out for Larissa's good. "I have heard it said Lady Dorothea is not exactly the trustworthy sort."

Larissa's eyes shot open. "Now I know you're jealous." She pointed an accusing finger at him.

He took the hand she had proffered in anger and held it.

The look in her eyes softened, thawing into the customary warm glow with which she gazed at him for the duration of their conversations when they sat together in the library.

Randall wished he could hear the soothing caress of her voice instead of the harsh tones of reproach. Staring into her eyes, he saw her mirroring his own feelings.

Larissa's gaze swept to the door and she pulled her hand from Randall's. "Dorothea!"

His pleasant memory was lost. With Dorothea's presence, Larissa resumed her distant and cool manner. Randall did not know if he would see the compassionate side of Larissa he so loved ever again.

"Only passing through," Lord Firth said to all, explaining his unexpected presence. He had arrived just in time for that evening's supper and sat down with Melton and the other guests. The gentlemen did not tarry in the dining room long and soon roamed into the parlor with their glasses of port in hand.

Melton paced in front of the empty hearth. He shifted the glass from hand to hand, swirling its contents. "Tell us, Firth, you seem in high dudgeon this evening. What's bothering you?"

"I don't find fault with a fat goose for nothing, Melton," Firth grumbled. "A fortnight ago, I was waylaid by a highwayman."

Lady Brookhurst gave a gasp. Dorothea moved to her mother's side and took her hand for comfort. Apparently, Lady Brookhurst was of a delicate constitution.

"Dastardly deed, it was. Can't seem to shake it. He dressed all in black and wore a black tricorn, shading the mask that covered his eyes."

Lady Brookhurst clasped the pearl strand around her neck and gave a horrific gasp.

In an ominous tone, the marquess continued, "That's what I've heard from Lord and Lady Greenleigh, held up last week. Coming up to town, you understand. Stopped them just outside London. Black waistcoat, black shirt, black breeches, black greatcoat and Hessians. The only bit of color on him was an unusual stick pin. Gold with engraved initials, if I'm not mistaken."

"Initials? What initials?" Firth demanded.

"I believe Greenleigh said it was T. R. F. if I'm not mistaken."

"T. R. F.? That's *my* bloody stickpin," Firth roared. "By gad, I want to see that scoundrel swing."

Lady Brookhurst gave a great caterwaul, slumping into the back of the sofa.

"Maman, are you all right? Do get some sherry, please," Dorothea asked William. She held the proffered sherry to her mother's lips. "Here Maman, just take a sip." This seemed to restore Lady Brookhurst for she looked quite recovered.

"That's not the half of it," Melton added, his eyes bugging out of his head as he worked his disastrous tale. "He beckoned Greenleigh's daughter near for a kiss."

"So after he's taken the riches he wants, he's after the girls?" Firth was outraged. He downed his port in one swallow.

"Ravaging the ladies!" Lady Brookhurst cried in fright.

Again, Dorothea raised the sherry to her mother's lips for a medicinal dose.

William gave a polite cough into his fist, trying to hide his skeptical grin.

"He wears Hessians, you say. Could he be a man of quality?" Dorothea whispered in the same dark manner.

"How could that be?" Lady Brookhurst queried in disbelief. "A real gentleman would never lower himself."

"My, I certainly hope he can live up to this reputation of his," William replied, giving a chuckle.

"It's not a laughing matter." Larissa cast him a dark look. "It's simply dreadful."

"What you don't realize, Lady Trent, is there's always a highwayman lurking somewhere. Some get caught, some give it up, and some continue from year to year." William eased back in the chair, propped his feet up and held his glass, inspecting its contents. "Horrid way to make a living. Far too dangerous for my taste. Bound to get shot one of these days, and if you're caught, hanged."

"They've gone without us again," Larissa huffed in exasperation the next afternoon.

"You must get used to it," Lady Brookhurst said. "When out and about in the country, the gentlemen busy themselves out-of-doors, and we ladies must entertain ourselves."

Larissa had never been to a country house. She did not realize the activities of men and women were segregated.

"The lady of the house usually attends to such things, but—" Lady Brookhurst gestured to her daughter. "Dorothea here, could step in, could you not?"

"Maman," Dorothea censured in a tone of disapproval.

"Come now, my dear, you are here at his lordship's insistence," Lady Brookhurst pointed out. "The marquess is quite taken with Dorothea," she said to Larissa. "I do not think it would be too soon to say she is in line to be the next marchioness."

"Maman, please," Dorothea chided. "Larissa and I were just on our way out."

"We were?" she whispered to Dorothea who immediately led Larissa out of the parlor.

Their premature departure prevented an embarrassing scene from becoming more so. "We are going driving," Dorothea announced. "And I shall drive."

"You know how to drive?" Larissa gasped.

"Oh, yes," Dorothea exclaimed. "Every lady must learn to be truly self-sufficient. Don't tell me Sir Randall would have any objections to your learning?"

"No, I'm sure he has none at all. It's only that I . . . I had never thought of taking on such a task."

"Mark my words, you'll learn in no time at all."

Once the curricle was in motion, Dorothea simply handed the ribbons over to Larissa. At first she felt nervous, but once she adjusted to the pull of the horses against the wide leather ribbons, driving the team was not so bad at all. As a matter of fact, not only was it easier than she had expected, it was very enjoyable.

Larissa wasn't sure if it was the feeling of independence or the feeling of speed. Why, she was moving barely at a trot and a slow one at that.

The curricle was small and at one point Larissa had lifted a wheel rounding a corner. It was then she realized how hazardous it would be to race along at breakneck speeds as she had heard some young men did for a wager.

By the end of their ride, Larissa's hands were sore. Next time she would wear heavier gloves. She wasn't sure how or why, but something told her there would indeed be a next time.

Chapter Twenty

The following morning Lord Melton and his guest, Lord Firth, met up with William and Randall at the stables. The marquess gestured for the younger men to join them.

"We met with Lord Ardsmore out in the south pasture. He was on his way to Carswell to tell us he was robbed last night. He's most upset. Most upset."

"Understandably so," Randall agreed.

"He's still planning to go ahead with his dinner tonight. Too late to call it off without turning people away at the door. That would be dashed bad form, you know."

"Was it the same blighter?" Firth quizzed.

"He said the highwayman wielded two Italian dueling pistols. He could see the silver handles glinting in the moonlight, along with the stickpin at his throat.

"Adding to the rumor he is of quality, Ardsmore says he speaks in the most elegant of tones." Melton stared at

Firth while relaying the unpleasant news. "I don't want to worry the ladies any."

"It'd start their imaginations spiraling," William whispered to Randall. One side of William's mouth turned upward, giving a half smile. "Women find stolen kisses from a highwayman exciting, don't you know."

"Ardsmore's called in the Runners," Melton explained. "Offered a bonus to catch the blackguard who bussed his new wife."

"Bussin' Billy, they call him," Firth added.

"Bussin' Billy, a bit common for a supposed nob, wouldn't you say?" William interjected. From his brother's hard stare, Randall knew the opinion was an unwelcome one.

"The point is"—Melton continued, clearing his throat—"the man's not dangerous. He's not leaving a trail of bodies behind."

"That's a relief," William added. "He'll only steal my valuables."

"Dash it, Wills," Randall chided. "What could be more valuable than your life?"

"Ardsmore went after Billy with the concealed knife in his cane. Made sorry work of the blighter's greatcoat. Slashed a fair portion of fabric under his arm."

"Why couldn't his blasted aim have been better?" Firth criticized.

"Avoiding the mortal blow, Billy stumbled back to the edge of the stream. This time of year it's just a trickle of water. He merely muddied his Hessians."

Randall knew by the look on Firth's face he gained

some small measure of satisfaction knowing the highwayman had ruined the finish on an expensive pair of boots.

"And it gives the Runners one more clue to his identity," Melton concluded.

"That is good news," William agreed.

Melton and Firth went ahead to the house. William snagged Randall's arm, holding him back for a few words.

"I might as well let it be known I plan on keeping my distance from the new Lady Ardsmore," William admitted. "Had dealings with her myself. She is most comely." William hiked his eyebrows in a favorable expression. "It's all dashedly awkward now that she lives just over at the next piece of property and married to Ardsmore no less." William tossed the stalk he'd been chewing onto the ground before exiting the barn.

"It's that bad, is it?" Randall mused.

"It does not bode well for me, I'll say that much." William tossed the hay to the ground.

"Then I take it you won't be joining us this evening."

"Not on your life," he professed. "I don't mean to belittle the situation, but really." William chuckled. "I think Terrance is afraid Bussin' Billy will kiss Dorothea before he'll ever have a chance."

Randall suspected that given the opportunity Dorothea might find it thrilling to be in the arms of a dangerous highwayman.

He entered the house in time to hear the butler announce to Lord Melton, "It's a Mr. Daniel Lawrence of the Bow Street Runners, my lord."

"What?" Melton looked behind Jenkins to the stranger

approaching in the hall. "I can't believe I, or any one in my house, could be suspected."

"My apologies, Lord Melton." Mr. Lawrence gave a deep bow from the waist. "I have my orders. We are conducting a search within a fifty-mile radius of the crime. The occupants found in every household and establishment are to be questioned about their whereabouts of last night." His gaze swept the faces of the occupants, searching for a telltale sign or hint of deception. "I need not conduct a search of the premises unless I feel there to be sufficient cause to do so."

Lord Melton could not contest the Runner's authority in the matter and had to concede. "The parlor is at your disposal."

"You are most gracious," Mr. Lawrence replied.

"Not at all." Melton gestured for the butler, who appeared at his side. "Jenkins, you will assist Mr. Lawrence with anything he might need."

"Yes, your lordship."

"If you will excuse me," Melton gestured with the flourish of his riding crop, "I shall return momentarily after I change."

"Lord Melton," Lawrence summoned the earl before he could ascend the grand staircase. "Would you be so kind as to be the first? It would make an excellent example for your guests."

Melton glanced around. "Of course," he said with a smile, ready to give his full cooperation, and headed in the direction of the front parlor.

Lawrence addressed the guests before following after

the marquess. "I'd appreciate if you didn't leave just now. Jenkins, please make sure everyone remains belowstairs until I've had the chance to speak to them."

"Just as you say, sir," Jenkins replied. Addressing the ensemble he continued, "If you gentlemen would be so good as to move into the breakfast room to wait, I shall see to it fresh coffee and tea are served."

William and Randall being the closest, they stepped into the room. Lord Firth followed, grumbling under his breath, "I'll expect something bloody well stronger than tea."

It was more than an hour later, and Randall was the last to be questioned. Not an unexpected outcome. After all, he was the lowest ranking of the guests. Completing the interview with Mr. Lawrence, he stood in the opened doorway to the parlor.

"I'm afraid your lack of alibi requires I take further steps. I will need to search your room."

Dorothea appeared from around the corner. "May I speak?" She held her clasped hands in front of her and looked down, studying the whitened knuckles.

Randall noted the baffled look on Mr. Lawrence's face and made the introductions.

"I only hesitate to come forward because of the delicate nature of the circumstance," she began. Dorothea looked up, greeting Mr. Lawrence's gaze with her wide blue eyes. "I do feel it is the only right thing to do."

The Bow Street Runner vowed, "I can assure you, I shall be most discreet with any information you divulge."

"Very well," Dorothea sighed, managing to overcome her reluctance. She followed the Runner into the parlor at a sedate pace. Mr. Lawrence gestured for Randall to join them and isolated the three of them behind closed doors.

"I believe Sir Randall told you he was in the library last night," Dorothea began.

"Yes, he did," Mr. Lawrence confirmed.

"He was not alone. I was with him."

Mr. Lawrence gave Randall a hardened look. "What do you mean you were 'with' him?"

"After the guests had retired for the evening, I came belowstairs to retrieve my book of Byron's poems. I had thought I left it in the drawing room. As it happens, Sir Randall had intercepted it and used it to lure me into the library." She stopped and moistened her lips between eyeing Mr. Lawrence's expression at regular intervals. "Need I go into detail?"

"It would be helpful if you could be a bit more specific," he said, urging her on, remaining very professional in his questioning.

"When I entered the room, Sir Randall stood in front of the closed door. I did not wish to wake anyone and cause a scene. He begged me to take the book from him, but held it just out of reach. The only way to retrieve it would be to put my arms around him. I was willing to leave the volume in his care and return to my room, but he would not take no for an answer." She paused again, the color in her face heightened. "I may as well tell you, sir, my mother and I are the guests of Lord Melton, and Sir Randall *is* a married man."

"All right," Mr. Lawrence stopped her, hearing enough. "When was this?"

"It must have been about an hour after everyone had re-tired. Ten o'clock, ten-thirty perhaps."

Without a change in his serious demeanor, Lawrence's gaze locked onto Randall. "You're free to go."

Hearing this slanderous tale Randall threw open the double doors.

Larissa, wearing a look of concern, stood in the hall-way with Melton, Firth, and William behind her. Mr. Lawrence stepped in front of Randall and announced, "I had a question about Sir Randall's whereabouts."

Larissa stepped forward, raising her chin. "He was with me last night." She knew it was a lie and couldn't help from blushing, but hoped it would be enough to convince Mr. Lawrence.

"I appreciate your attempt to protect him. After all, you are his wife." Mr. Lawrence made a nervous glance to-ward the now emerging Dorothea and cleared his throat. "Your husband has already been cleared. Lady Dorothea has already vouched for his innocence."

Randall noted a subtle look of betrayal spread on Larissa's face. Her hardened glare slid from Dorothea to him. He couldn't let her believe what she was thinking now. He could well imagine it was the worst she could concoct, and Randall knew she had quite the imagination.

Leading Larissa abovestairs and into the privacy of his room, Randall closed the door. He would explain, then force her to listen to reason. "I wish to inform you lest you hear this from another, more unsavory source."

Larissa kept silent.

"Dorothea claims I was in the midst of seducing her."

"Well that's it, isn't it?" Larissa addressed him with her

arms crossed and eyes ablaze. "You're not *really* married to me. You can do as you well please."

Along with the fury he felt inside, it gave him a strange sense of satisfaction that Lady Dorothea's phony alibi bothered Larissa.

"Do you think so little of me? Do you think I would insult you by seducing another while married to you? I have already promised you. While we are 'married,' I would prove to be the model husband."

"If that is true and you did not try to seduce her last night, what do you make of Dorothea's explanation?"

"I have no idea. How am I to explain her actions? Everything she said was completely untrue." Something in Larissa's wary stare told him of her doubts. He was not about to let her call him a liar. "You're the one who told them about us being together last night." He flung his hands up. "Maybe *I* did lie about last night. Maybe I did hold up Lord Ardsmore. Go ahead. Why don't you search my wardrobe for the damaged greatcoat and soiled boots." He led her to his dressing room by the arm and flung the door open. "It should be simple, I only have but a single pair of Hessians."

To his amazement, Larissa took him up on his offer and did just that. With her chin held high, she went in to see for herself.

Was he really so untrustworthy? After she finished rummaging through his wardrobe, she would feel the thorough fool.

Randall had decided he'd be gracious and accept whatever apology she offered. No use causing problems when they had near a month remaining in their "marriage." He could be accepting, giving, and accommodating more than most, he surmised.

It was only when Larissa reappeared in the doorway with a coat draped over one arm and a pair of muddied Hessians in the other that he felt his legs give way beneath him and he dropped onto his bed.

Chapter Twenty-one

"Where did you find those?" The shock on Sir Randall's face was genuine.

"In your wardrobe, just as you said."

"They're not mine." It was a reflexive response on his part. He stood and approached the incriminating garments, taking a second look. "They *are* mine. I don't know how they have come to be in this condition."

Sir Randall took the coat and rummaged through the folds. He was not disappointed. There it was, just as Lord Melton had described. The telltale tear on the right side under the arm, a clean, precise cut presumably made by a knife.

He stepped back and sank onto the bed again. "If Lawrence had the notion to search my room . . ."

"This would have looked very bad for you."

He massaged his throat. "I would have been hanged by the end of the week."

185

The thought of Sir Randall swinging at the end of a rope made Larissa feel faint. "Who would have done such a thing?" She sank onto the bed beside him. "If the stolen items had been found in your possession, I have no doubt the authorities would have done just that."

"Do you think whoever framed me might have also planted the stolen jewelry in my room?" Sir Randall did not wait for a reply, but scrambled to the small table next to his bed, pulling open the drawers. He finished the search of his side table and leaped to his feet to search through the clothespress and desk.

"They must think you more clever than to simply hide them under a few shirts or waistcoats." Larissa watched disbelief overtake the look of terror on his face.

He paused and straightened. "Do you really think so?"

"On second thought, I cannot imagine they would think you that intelligent."

"That's a fairly insensitive thing to say. But it's not you who is being framed is it?" An insulted expression crossed Sir Randall's face. "It would be nice to know you're concerned."

"I am concerned," she said, not wanting to confess her feelings outright. "That is why I am willing to repair the tear in your coat. I suggest you clean your boots before Mr. Lawrence changes his mind and searches the house." She took up the greatcoat and headed for her room.

Sir Randall caught her arm, delaying her. "You do care, don't you?" he whispered and smiled.

Larissa gripped the torn greatcoat a little tighter and

looked into his eyes. If he felt for her as she did for him, she need not answer that question.

"Where have you been all morning?" Dorothea asked Larissa when she came into the breakfast room.

"I'm afraid I must have lost track of the time. I was in my room, busy sewing."

"Why do you look at me so, Larissa?" Dorothea asked, sounding quite hurt. "I thought we were friends."

"Friends do not steal husbands from one another," Larissa snapped.

"Please, not so loud," Dorothea hushed, rose from the table and neared, beckoning Larissa into a coze. "You want to know why I said what I did about Sir Randall?"

She did not respond, and kept her features schooled into an emotionless mask.

"I did it *because* of our friendship," Dorothea professed.

"You can't possibly expect me to believe that."

"Why else would I tell such a lie? To give Sir Randall an alibi of course."

"What?" This piece of news brought Larissa around.

"The Runners would think his wife would lie for him. They might even expect it. But for me to claim he was with me should prove shocking to say the least. Scandalous if it should be heard publicly. So I lied to keep him above suspicion. I might as well tell you the truth, I saw him strolling about outside alone."

Larissa didn't know what to say. Dorothea's little white lie had kept him safe. Most of all, she prevented Mr. Lawrence from taking his search above stairs to Sir

Randall's closet, where, it was certain, the runner would have found irrefutable evidence of his guilt. Only, Larissa knew Sir Randall could not have done it.

"Of course, he could not have done it," Dorothea continued. "I should never believe him capable of such action."

"What you have shown me proves your actions have gone beyond those of mere friendship." Larissa smiled. "Please accept my apology, Dorothea. How could I have ever thought ill of you?"

"I am only too happy to avoid problems between Sir Randall and the law." Dorothea seemed to have been genuinely relieved. "I hope I haven't caused any difficulties between the two of you."

"No, you have not."

"It must be ever so reassuring to have the love of such a trustworthy man."

"It is something I cannot begin to explain," Larissa said, stating the unequivocal truth.

That evening, Larissa entered the parlor. Dorothea and Lady Brookhurst were there waiting to leave for Ardsmore Lodge.

"Oh, the men always make light of the ladies taking their time, but faith, will you look at who is waiting for the gentlemen." Lady Brookhurst gestured about her with her silk fan. She stilled, fixing a critical eye on Larissa. "How lovely you look, except . . . except . . ."

"Is there something amiss?" Larissa looked down at her gown. Her hands moved from her skirts to the curls atop her head, wondering if her hair was out of place.

"She is perfection itself, Maman," Dorothea praised. Her fingers came to rest on her gold locket.

Glancing at her neckline, Larissa had also suspected the décolletage too low for good taste. With the look on Lady Brookhurst's face, Larissa must have been right.

"I have it!" Lady Brookhurst's face lit up.

"Have Regina fetch my garnets," she said to her daughter. Within minutes, Regina returned with a beautiful wooden inlaid decorated box. Lady Brookhurst drew out a garnet necklace and held it to Larissa's gown. "This will go splendidly with your gown. They are not grand by any stretch of the imagination, but I imagine they should do."

Lady Brookhurst told Regina to lay the necklace around Larissa's neck, then fasten the bracelet around her wrist.

"What an improvement, do you not think, dear?"

"Maman, you are so right as always," Dorothea replied.

"Wearing colored gems is one of the small pleasures of being married."

After admiring the dark stones encircling her wrist, Larissa laid a hand at her throat, touching the necklace, wishing she could see them around her neck. "Thank you, Lady Brookhurst."

"Just make sure and return them when you've finished." Lady Brookhurst gave a regal nod and proceeded to check on the status of the men.

For some reason unknown to Larissa, she and Sir Randall were to travel separately, while Lady Brookhurst, Dorothea, and Melton traveled in his coach. Whether

Melton wished to be alone with Dorothea, expecting her mother to fall asleep, as she had a tendency to do in a moving vehicle, or whether Sir Randall had used the opportunity to arrange time alone with her, she could not say.

However, Larissa did find conversation between them somewhat awkward. Larissa found the easy exchange of words that once flowed between them gone, the need to be close to him and the harmonious feeling she once felt between them forgotten.

Or so she had thought.

Dinner at the Ardsmore's proceeded smoothly. No one dared bring up the recent robbery of their hosts. That was, until the ladies retired to the drawing room and Dorothea spoke.

"I do hope you have recovered from that unfortunate incident."

Larissa couldn't believe Dorothea's lack of decorum. How could she bring up such an unpleasant subject?

"Was Billy as handsome as they say?" Lady Brookhurst wanted to know.

"He was so handsome and strong, from what I could see. He wore that mask you know," Lady Ardsmore replied. "His lips tore the very breath from my body when he . . . kissed me. I should wish Ardsmore could have such an effect."

The ladies laughed, a mixture of outrage at her honest admission and envy. How could Lady Ardsmore have enjoyed being held up? Larissa wondered.

There was a part of Larissa that could perhaps understand the thrill of a robbery where no one was harmed, looking at it from the safety of hindsight. Three months ago, she might have reacted the same way herself. It was an adventure!

How she had grown from Miss Quinn, the innocent seminary girl, to Lady Trent, the baronet's worldly wife.

Larissa realized she was not the same person at all.

Chapter Twenty-two

This night had been just as warm as the last. A wisp of a cloud slipped in front of the night's full moon, illuminating the green of the plants into silver. Rounding the corner on this side of the crossroads to Marsgate, the horses gave a great protest when Sir Randall brought the rig to a halt.

"Stand and deliver!" announced the booming baritone of a highwayman dressed in black who occupied the middle of the road atop a black horse. The black mount pranced in a carefully guided tight circle. Bussin' Billy kept his primed pistol leveled upon his prey. "I'll be relieving you of those gems, my lady."

Larissa's hand drew to her neck, fingering Lady Brookhurst's garnet necklace before working the clasp loose and dropping it followed by the bracelet, into her lap.

"You, sir, stay seated. I'll ask you, my lady, to step down, if you will." Keeping his attention keen on Sir Randall,

Bussin' Billy dismounted. "If you please, my lord, your valuables and any monetary sums you may have on your person, hand them to your lovely companion."

Sir Randall removed his fob from his waistcoat, pulled out his watch, unfastened his gold studs from his cuffs and pulled out his ruby stickpin from the folds of his cravat, handing them to Larissa one by one.

"Here, my fair lady, I await a kiss from your sweet lips." Keeping the pistol aimed at Sir Randall, Billy held out his other hand for Larissa.

Sir Randall nudged her forward. "Go ahead, you know he won't harm you."

Larissa stepped toward the highwayman, preparing herself for the completion of the ritual by delivering a kiss one might bestow upon a hero instead of a scoundrel. She leaned toward him, the same scent of spice Sir Randall wore wafted from his cape.

Instead of pulling her close, Bussin' Billy took hold of her arm and tucked it behind her waist, holding her steady against him. He then took quick but careful aim at Sir Randall and pulled the trigger.

The pistol spit fire. A blast ripped through the air, echoing through the night. Larissa could feel the reverberation in her chest. A small grey cloud of smoke drifted past between her and the stricken Sir Randall, who fell back against the seat.

Larissa screamed, somehow managed to struggle free, and ran back to the curricle to Sir Randall's aid. He lay on the seat, his wounded arm draped onto the floor. He might have looked as if he were asleep, except for the growing dark stain on the sleeve of his expensive jacket.

The movement of the horses nearly caused Larissa to lose her balance. Then the rig lurched forward, sending her toppling over Sir Randall's leg. She landed on the seat next to him.

The horses bolted, carrying the occupants of the transport for an uncontrolled ride. Larissa grasped for the ribbons, sliding from their loose tether. She managed to gain hold of them and pulled back as hard as she could.

"Stop! Stop! Oh, please stop!" Larissa stood on her feet, leaning back with all her might, to no avail. The horses ran on.

Sir Randall must have recovered, for the next thing she knew, his hand came over hers and applied the added effort needed to stop the bolting team. Exhausted, he fell against the squabs.

She secured the ribbons and bent to Sir Randall's side. "I was scared to death. I thought he might have killed you."

"Might have killed me? I knew you would be rid of me, but—are you disappointed?" Larissa helped Sir Randall sit upright.

"What a horrible thing to say. I would never wish you dead."

"Well that's nice to hear," he managed, gasping for air. She could see perspiration dotted along his forehead and upper lip. His usual warm expressive eyes were now vacant and mirrored pain.

"Does it hurt much? Let me see," Larissa offered. She winced at the sight of the wound, keeping her touch as light as possible. She lifted his jacket and pulled it off his shoulder.

"Bloody hell!" he cried through his teeth.

The sleeve of his once smartly tailored jacket lay torn and soaked with blood. The flesh on his arm Larissa once knew as smooth was torn, looking angry and raw.

"It hurts enough," he groaned through clenched teeth.

"I must bind your arm to stop the bleeding." Larissa lifted the hem of her gown and tore at her white underskirt. She noticed he chanced a peek at her stocking-clad limbs. "Really, Sir Randall." She threw the hem of her gown over her knees bringing his diversion to an end. "You're in no position to make a game of this. You're seriously hurt."

"No one knows that better than I. You can't begrudge me something to ease the pain."

"You'll find that in no way will staring at my garters ease your pain."

"Oh, I don't know," he mused. A gentle smile warmed his ashen face. "I seem to think my pain has lessened somewhat."

She pressed a pad onto the wound. "Hold this," she instructed. She wrapped his upper arm with the longest strip and pulled the material taut.

"Ouch! Would you please take care!"

"Sorry." She winced in sympathy. Larissa pressed her hand against his face. His skin was cool to the touch, moist and clammy. She draped his coat over him for warmth before she took up the ribbons.

Lucky for her, Dorothea had insisted she try her hand at driving a team. Now she could manage to get them home.

On the way home, Larissa realized how easily she had escaped from Bussin' Billy. And how did they become unwilling passengers of the runaway rig into the dead of night?

The highwayman must have allowed her to run back to the curricle. He could have quite easily prevented her from leaving his side. Why did he let her go?

Turning up the long drive, Carswell Castle loomed ahead, looking magical in the moonlight. Larissa knew Sir Randall needed care as soon as possible, but slowed the horse to navigate over the narrow bridge spanning the moat. Once inside the fortress walls, she followed the gravel path to the main house.

Up ahead parked next to the house was a black phaeton. To her knowledge it was not one Lord Melton owned.

Sir Randall's eyes opened to narrow slits, managing a brief look. "Thank God the doctor's here," he slurred before his head lulled back on the squabs.

"The doctor?" She looked at Sir Randall and laid a protective hand on his shoulder. Something was wrong, she could feel it. Larissa slowed the horses to give herself time to ponder the conundrum set before her.

She still could not comprehend why the doctor was there. True, Sir Randall needed a physician, but how had it happened one had arrived? No one at the Castle could have known of Sir Randall's plight. The doctor must have been called to attend to someone else. Exactly what had happened for someone to need a doctor? Larissa would not allow Sir Randall or herself to be lured into a trap. The situation called for caution, and careful she would be.

"We're back at the castle." She roused Sir Randall. "It's time to go in."

"What?" he groaned, lifting his head.

"Can you manage to walk into the house?"

A smile waned across his face. "If I can hold onto you for support, I'm sure I can manage." He pushed himself upright to disembark.

Larissa pulled his greatcoat over his shoulders, covering the traces of his injury.

"You might need to steady me. I'm not sure how well I am able to remain upright."

"That's all right." She coaxed him closer, slipping her right arm around his back, taking some of his weight. "Just lean on me as much as you need." Larissa could feel the rise and fall of his chest as he breathed.

"How are you to explain my condition?"

"I imagine I shall think of something." It was the least of her worries. What concerned her more was what awaited her inside. With Sir Randall draped over her shoulder, Larissa moved forward.

The front door opened and they entered.

With the light of the foyer, she could see the loss of blood had made Sir Randall pale. The Marquess of Melton and Lord William emerged from the parlor. The trill of Lady Brookhurst rang through the hall, permeating the air.

"What has happened?" Larissa asked. The shock on her face could only be equaled by the shock on Lord William's when he saw Sir Randall.

"We've been held up by Bussin' Billy." Lord Melton mopped his brow with a handkerchief.

"Was anyone hurt?" she asked, concerned beyond measure since Sir Randall had been wounded.

"Lady Brookhurst is suffering from spasms, the physician is attending to her now." Lord Melton pocketed his fine linen handkerchief. "It was Dorothea," the marquess explained. "The scoundrel called her for a buss and she shot the cur. Had a pistol hidden in her muff. It was horrible! Horrible! I saw it all with my own two eyes."

As if on cue, Dorothea emerged from the parlor, joining them.

"Dorothea was so brave. She saved us all!" He planted a kiss on her outstretched hand.

Dorothea seemed quite calm with all that had happened. Her wide eyes inspected Sir Randall's crumpled form. "Whatever is the matter with Sir Randall?"

"Nothing nearly so tragic. He has once again overindulged." Larissa gave him a loving glance. "I best get him off to bed."

"Let me give you a hand," Lord William offered. He took up Sir Randall's left side and bore most of the baronet's weight up the stairs. Larissa sensed Lord William's confusion.

Sir Randall had been adamant about their friendship. Larissa knew he could be trusted. Lord William remained quiet until they had reached the privacy of Sir Randall's room.

They laid the groaning Sir Randall onto his bed. His head lulled back and half fell onto his pillow. It was not the look of someone who's drunk deep. He had the look of someone who had lost a lot of blood.

Lord William retrieved the light as Larissa made Sir Randall comfortable.

"What ails him?" Lord William asked. Something in his voice told Larissa he hadn't believed the drinking tale, and now he wanted the truth.

Larissa gave a somber stare and drew aside Sir Randall's greatcoat, revealing a large red stain on his right arm.

"My God, he's been shot! I'll get the doctor. I'm sure he hasn't left yet."

"No!" Larissa grabbed Lord William's sleeve before he could get away.

"Why on earth not?"

"It's all so confusing, so complicated." Larissa could not prevent her tears from spilling. "I don't think they believe what happened to him. Don't you think it's a bit peculiar Sir Randall and Bussin' Billy were shot on the same night and in the same place?"

"It would seem that someone would want him mistaken for the highwayman." Lord William stood his ground. "Do you have proof to indicate otherwise?"

"You know it isn't true." She loosened Sir Randall's cravat. "Please, you must help me."

Lord William drew his pocket knife and sliced the Weston masterpiece away, exposing the bloodied shirt from the wound. He rolled Sir Randall onto his side to examine his arm. The ball had torn a good chunk of his flesh away, but had not hit the bone. "If we clean the wound and keep him still, he should be all right."

Lord William moved to the dressing table and dispensed a portion of water into the basin. He slid aside something and set the pitcher down when he finished. Returning to the bed he handed a clean towel to Larissa who had finished removing the blood-caked bandage.

"I don't know if you'll ever believe me. We were held up," Larissa explained. "The highwayman, it was Bussin' Billy. He stole the necklace and bracelet loaned to me by Lady Brookhurst and he took Sir Randall's pocket watch and ruby stickpin."

Lord William glanced over his shoulder, straightened and returned to the dressing table. "You mean these?" Lord William held out his hand displaying several glittering objects. A ruby stickpin, gold studs, and a watch.

Larissa began to feel faint. "It's impossible, they were stolen." Her words came out in a gasp.

"Apparently, they have managed to find their way home."

Larissa did not know whether Lord William believed her or not, but he did not hold disbelief in his voice. "Do you suppose Lady Brookhurst's jewels have returned as well?"

"I cannot imagine why not," William drawled with trepidation. "Shall I inquire?"

"No," Larissa answered in a quick burst. "We must see to Randall first." A strange feeling came over her. Perhaps she was going mad. She could not have imagined the horrible events of that evening.

"Ah, yes, ministrations to the needy." He looked down at his friend, to the affected arm in particular, at different angles. "It's taken out a good chunk but there's no lead in there. We'll need to cauterize that wound, though." Lord William seemed to know exactly what to do.

"Won't he cry out?" Larissa didn't need the entire household coming to his aid.

"No, we'll lose him before he gets around to screaming."

My, he was taking all this casually. "What do you want me to do?"

"Get the brandy, we'll need to give him some tolerance first." Larissa brought back the decanter and a glass while he propped Sir Randall up onto the pillows. Lord William held the glass while Larissa poured. He positioned himself next to his friend. "He isn't pretty when he's been drinking," Lord William said, dribbling the brandy down Sir Randall's throat.

Sir Randall tried to resist the alcohol.

"Thank you for the warning." At least that was one aspect she had been spared, until now.

After several healthy swallows of the potent spirit, in addition to his present condition, Sir Randall had quite lost all his self-restraint and had begun a stream of incoherent babbling.

"Ah, Larissa . . ." he beckoned. "Come sit by me, my sweet."

With a quick, unsettling glance to Lord William she approached the bed. Sir Randall reached out and took her hand, drawing her near. She hoped Sir Randall would not say anything to embarrass either one of them.

He covered the back of her hand with kisses, then rubbed it against his cheek. "How I've dreamed of us like this, so many times." Then pressed her hand to his cheek.

"Me, lying next to you?" she whispered in half amusement and half surprise.

"Only you are wrapped in my arms."

Larissa watched the strain on his face in an attempt to lift his injured arm and bring it around her.

"And just as in my dreams. Some force beyond my control prevents me from moving to do so." He gave a dramatic groan, displaying his futility. "I am a complete ass," Sir Randall willingly announced. "I was born one."

"And you'll always be one. I've never had a doubt," Lord William concluded in hopes of ending the patient's ramblings. "Now keep quiet and lie still. This will hurt plenty."

"I've always hated you, Wills," Randall snarled at his friend.

"I know. You'd do the exact same for me, I wager."

"You bet I would," Randall responded, unaware of what was about to happen to him.

"He's as ready as he'll ever be." Lord William moved to the hearth and placed the poker into the flames, heating the element. "Open the windows," he said. "We're going to need some fresh air."

Larissa pulled aside the heavy drawn drapes, threw open the windows and returned to the bed.

"Lay across his body and hold his good arm down tight," Lord William instructed.

Larissa did as he asked and laid across his torso, pinning his good arm down with both her hands. In his inebriated state, Sir Randall's head rolled to one side. His alcohol-glazed eyes stared into Larissa's face.

"You s-smell s-so good," Sir Randall whispered to Larissa. "Some men would do anything to be this close to a beautiful lady."

"I wish you would stop this nonsense, you're seriously hurt." If only he had not been foxed when he said that.

Lord William drew the red hot poker from the fire and approached the bed. He used his knee to hold his friend down, took a deep breath, and pressed the heated poker into the wound.

Chapter Twenty-three

It only took a few seconds.

A sickening hissing sound mingled with the putrid odor of burning flesh permeated the air. As Lord William predicted, Sir Randall fell unconscious before crying out.

Larissa leaped off the bed and ran to the window, gasping for fresh air. "What are we to do about the smell?" she managed between gulps of fresh air.

"It will clear." Lord William's face contorted in a dreadful mask, waving the smell away with his hand. He turned Sir Randall to his side and completed the treatment, sending a second wave of noxious fumes into the room.

Again Larissa leaned out of the casement, purging her lungs of the horrid smell.

"Not before questions are asked," she pointed out. How would they explain the stench? The answer came to her. She left Sir Randall's room through the connecting doors.

She returned from her room with a pair of scissors and handed them to Lord William.

One by one, she removed the pins from her head. Her hair tumbled down past her shoulders. Lord William regarded her actions with a quizzical eye and stared at the cold metal tool in his hand.

"What do you want me to do with these?" he said, brandishing the scissors.

"I want you to cut my hair, here." She indicated at shoulder length.

"What?" he balked, setting them on the table. "What bird-witted start are you up to now?"

Larissa spun to face him. "To explain the smell, of course. This stench won't be gone by morning. I'll tell the servants that in his inebriated condition, Sir Randall cut my hair and burned the locks."

"Ah," Lord William brightened, spotting her reasoning. "Capital idea," he brightened.

"But I will need some help." She handed the scissors, handle first, again to Lord William, who accepted. "I cannot manage by myself."

Larissa held up most of her hair, allowing a fine layer to hang down her back. Slicing through her hair, he removed the long, cut section and laid it aside on the table. Layer by layer, he followed the previously cut length until all her hair fell just short of her shoulders.

"I've done a ghastly thing," he said, noting his work.

"Nonsense, you've most likely saved Sir Randall's life."

Larissa gathered the cut hair and scattered a small portion over the fire. The hair shriveled in the heat and added to the dreadful smell, leaving small curly remnants to serve as evidence. "That should suffice. We only need enough to explain the smell, there's no need to add to it."

"Randall will draw my cork for ruining your mane. And by the bye, what do you plan to do with the remainder?"

"You shouldn't worry, I shall place it where no one will ever find it."

"I'll likely be held for aiding a criminal and for telling such a bounder in the first place."

"Lord William, I think you worry too much." Larissa walked her accomplice to the door and saw him out. "Just leave the rest to me." She glanced at Sir Randall resting in his bed and fingered the blunt edges of her newly shorn hair.

It was her sincerest hope that in the end all would set itself to right.

Before settling herself in a chair at Sir Randall's side for the night, Larissa removed the torn, bloodied sleeve of his jacket and hung the coat sleeve-side-out in the clothespress. If anyone should search, all would look as it should.

Larissa folded her locks and the bloody sleeves in the center of the pillow of the tapestry she had recently finished and began to stitch the last side closed. She would keep the pillow, and the evidence of last night would stay well hidden.

Throughout the night, the springs of Sir Randall's bed groaned under the strain of his restless sleep. She hoped fever would not take hold. He moaned countless times and even called out her name. She stayed by his side to keep him quiet and comfortable.

In the morning when Randall woke, his whole body

ached. He had drunk himself into only a few stupors in his life, but this time he had no doubt he had gone far beyond what he considered the norm. Besides the glass of wine with dinner and a few sips of port after, he didn't even recall drinking. His eyes cracked open and he tried to move.

Starting from his right shoulder, spreading out to his hand, there was pain. When he reached to massage it, he found a bandage covering his upper arm.

A glance at his surroundings told him he lay in his bedroom. Asleep in a chair by his bedside lay Larissa. "What's happened?" he rasped, feeling disoriented.

She moved to his side. Her hands pressed his cheeks and forehead as if he were ill. Randall inhaled her enticing fragrance of spring, freshness, and sunlight. Her voice whispered soft and gentle like mist on a passing breeze. Her lovely face hovered above him, calling him by name, beckoning him. He reached out and pulled her close.

"What happened?" His throat felt scratchy as he spoke.

"Do you not remember?"

"No. Nothing." His head hurt too much to even attempt the effort.

"The robbery? Getting shot? Stopping the runaway horses?"

Randall's hand fell from her. "Sounds as if I was quite the hero."

"Not exactly," she corrected, moving away from the bed.

He stared at Larissa. This was more than an alcohol-induced hallucination. There was something decidedly different about her. Yet it did not come to him at once.

"What has happened to your hair?"

A light flush came over Larissa's cheeks when she

reached up and fingered the loose tendrils about her head. With most of the length removed, her hair fell into soft curls, framing her face.

"I had Lord William cut my hair to explain the smell in your room."

"Smell?" Randall sniffed, trying to determine if a scent was present in his room. "I don't smell anything."

"We had to cauterize that nasty wound on your arm last night. It left quite a stench."

Randall felt the wound on his upper arm. It throbbed in pain.

Events of the previous night began to surface. The dinner at Ardsmore's. Driving home with Larissa. The robbery. Being shot. Taking a peek at her ankles. How could he have forgotten?

"How ever did we manage to return?" he asked.

"I drove the curricle."

"You?" How did she . . . how could she manage? Randall's head throbbed.

Without a knock, William entered and closed the door behind him. "Gad, you look a fright."

"And good morning to you as well," Randall replied in amusement. "How much of this are you involved in?"

"Only seeing you up to your room, getting you drunker than a lord, and acting as your doctor."

"So you're responsible. Why didn't you just let me die?" Between the pain emanating from his arm, the unbearable pounding in his head and the nausea caused by the drink, Randall did not feel much like living.

"You weren't that bad off," his friend assured him.

"Wouldn't have done it unless it was completely necessary." William crossed his arms and leaned against one of the bedposts in a cavalier fashion.

"So you say," Randall mused. "I have yet to reach the same conclusion myself."

"You have, my friend, given a whole new meaning to 'bloody nuisance!'" William chucked. "If you haven't heard yet, ole boy, Bussin' Billy was shot last night. And just by an unbelievable coincidence, he is reported to be wounded in exactly the same place as you."

"Bussin' Billy was shot in the right arm last night? *I* was shot in the right arm last night. Someone might mistake my coincidental injury and assume Bussin' Billy and I are one and the same."

"If they found out, I imagine Bow Street might jump to the very same conclusion."

"That doesn't sound much like a coincidence at all."

William glanced to the vigilant Larissa and remarked in a laconic tone, "You see, after all Randall has been through last night, he still remains sharp as ever."

"This is not a joking matter," Randall protested, bringing himself upright even though it pained him.

"You find, my dear friend, if you will take a closer look, I am not sporting a smile. Terrance is not going to look kindly upon this if he finds out." William gave a shrug. "I might suggest you put in an appearance belowstairs to dissuade suspicion."

"I've made the excuse you are feeling poorly," Larissa added. "Your appearance last night was enough to convince the others."

"I'll need help dressing," Randall smiled at Larissa, knowing she had no intention of lending a hand, or laying a hand on his person.

"Won't do for a lady to tie your cravat, don't you know," William interjected.

"You shan't have to face that problem," Larissa confessed. Her eyes were downcast and her voice hesitant. "I needed to bind your wound. I've already sacrificed one of my underskirts. I'm afraid I've used a few of your neckcloths as dressing."

"I only have a few." He sounded outraged. "How could you—"

"I suppose you could borrow some from Lord William, can you not?" She looked hopefully at William.

Randall grimaced. "I suppose it's not like asking to wear his small clothes is it?"

"We'll make do," William said. "Can't have my valet involved. The man couldn't keep a secret if his life depended on it." Randall knew his friend had resigned himself that he must lend a hand. "I suppose that leaves me."

Larissa left Lord William to aid Sir Randall with his morning toilet. Sir Randall had not appreciated all that she had done for him. To scold her for using his neckcloths for bandages! His life must certainly be worth more than a few strips of linen. That silly man!

Dorothea sat alone at the long table. "There you are!" The expression on her face matched the delight in her eyes when Larissa entered the room. "Where have you been? What's happened to your hair?"

"I am sorry I've taken so long, I suppose I lost track of

the time. I was in my room sewing." At least that much was true. Larissa had spent nearly the entire night finishing the embroidery, cutting out the pillow, and sealing the incriminating evidence into the cushion.

Larissa fingered her shorn locks and knew what she was about to say would be a complete lie. "Sir Randall had a bit too much to drink last night. I'm afraid he experienced a spark of inspiration. He thought he was a hairdresser."

"Oh, dear," Dorothea voiced in sympathy, but a smile emerged.

"I suppose I shouldn't humor him. Someday he may wish to be a modiste, then I shall really be in the briars."

"I would hate to imagine. He'll have you scandalously draped in gauze." Her laughter was quickly replaced by a stifled yawn.

Larissa poured herself a cup of tea and sat next to Dorothea. "How are you doing this morning and how is your mother?"

"I'm afraid I didn't sleep well. Must have been the robbery."

"I imagine it was very disturbing." Larissa tried her very best to behave as if nothing unusual had happened.

"And Maman is so out of sorts, she cannot leave her bed." Melancholy left Dorothea momentarily. "She wishes me to thank you for returning her jewels so promptly. She feels better knowing all her jewelry is safe and sound."

Larissa tried not to look shocked at the news of the return of Lady Brookhurst's stolen jewels. Strange things were happening. Larissa harbored an injured man and lied at every turn. Deception was not dreamy or romantic, it was laced with fear and danger. One wrong word could give her away. If she were not believed, it could cost Sir Randall his life.

With the afternoon came the return of Daniel Lawrence. Melton and Lawrence entered the breakfast room first, two uniformed officers trailed behind. The marquess was in the midst of explaining the actions following the robbery, after they had returned to Carswell Castle.

Melton paused and gave Randall a smile that bordered on a leer.

"Sir Randall," Lawrence acknowledged.

"Mr. Lawrence," Randall responded. He set his coffee cup down with his left hand, holding his right arm still by his side.

"I think you'll find Sir Randall a bit unresponsive this morning." Melton winked. Randall stood and moved to the opposite side of the table to join the men, keeping movement with his upper body to a minimum.

Lawrence raised his brows. Randall imagined he was suspicious of everyone and everything.

"My word," Lord Melton exclaimed. "You certainly do make a nuisance of yourself when you're bosky, don't you ole boy?" The marquess gave Randall a clap on his shoulder. The injured one.

Randall gave a roar of laugher to mask his pain and took a step away. Melton advanced.

"It's surprising when you consider you couldn't walk up to your own bed when you came home. Must have caught a second wind, hey?" The marquess smacked him a second time.

Randall cried out again, masking his pain with laughter.

Mr. Lawrence must have noticed Randall's odd movements. He took a step toward Randall and demanded, "I would ask you to remove your coat so I might examine your arm." He paused. "You may comply with my wishes or I shall have these gentlemen do so forcibly. Either way I shall have my curiosity satisfied."

Chapter Twenty-four

He had no choice. Randall obeyed, shrugging off his coat. With Lord Melton's hardy slaps, he knew the wound had opened and he had bled through his bandage onto his shirtsleeve. The red stain on his arm would be there for all to see.

"May I ask how you sustained such an injury?" Mr. Lawrence inquired.

"I don't believe this!" Melton cried, his face grew red with anger.

"I can assure you, you will find the answer very difficult to accept."

"The truth, Trent," Melton ordered.

"Please, Lord Melton, it is my job to ask the questions," Lawrence interrupted.

"I was shot by Bussin' Billy when he held us up last night."

"Preposterous," Melton roared, spitting his words.

"I'm afraid we will need to search your room." Lawrence nodded to the two uniformed men who took up their post on either side of Randall.

Randall had searched his room after his discovery of the torn jacket and muddied Hessians and found nothing then. However, he had not checked his room this morning. Were the newly stolen items hidden in his room now?

By the time Lawrence returned, Larissa, Dorothea, Lady Brookhurst, and Lord William had joined the gathering.

"I have not found the stolen items, but your particular injury is circumstantial evidence I cannot ignore. I must bring charges against you under the suspicion of highway robbery, masquerading as the highwayman, Bussin' Billy. You are under arrest."

"No, it is a mistake!" Tears began to pool in Larissa's eyes. She grabbed on to Randall's arm, tightening her hold as if it could prevent his apprehension.

"I'll see you hang for this, Trent!" Lord Melton exclaimed. "You stay under my roof, try to seduce my fiancée, and rob me blind!"

"Whether he is guilty or not is up to a judge to decide," Lawrence silenced Melton.

"You've put the saddle on the wrong horse," Randall claimed. One of the constables wrenched his arms from his side and pulled them to the front.

"There's been a mistake all right." Lord Melton leveled an accusing finger at Randall. "You've made it, Trent. Highway robbery is a criminal act, but stealing from your host goes far beyond the pale. Hanging's not good enough for you."

The second constable placed the manacles on Randall's wrists. The dirty, cold metal restraints locked with a sickening clink.

Lady Brookhurst, who stood at the top landing, gave a cry and folded to the floor.

"Maman!" Dorothea cried and rushed to her mother's side. "Bring the salts!"

"Take him away!" Lord Melton ordered. The officers, with Sir Randall between them, took a step toward the front door.

"Please," Randall pleaded. "A word to my wife before I leave."

Melton turned to his guests. "I will allow this for Lady Trent's sake, for it shall be the last time she may set eyes upon her husband if I have anything to say about the matter. Three minutes in the parlor. And make sure you don't lose sight of him!" he thundered at the soldiers.

Larissa led the way to the parlor. The constables ushered Randall in and stopped at the door, still in full sight of their prisoner. Randall kept his back to them, shielding her from view.

"You are innocent!" she professed, keeping her voice to a whisper. "You cannot let them take you away."

He shrugged, raising his manacled wrist. "As you see there is little I can do." He took her trembling hands into his. "I'm afraid there is someone who feels they have a serious score to settle with me."

"But who? Why?"

"I don't know. And I don't know if I ever will discover the reason." This might be the last time he'd see her. He wanted to tell her how much she meant to him. "I am only sorry there is not time for—" Mere words felt inadequate. "I wanted you to know what I feel for you—" His voice strained, he could not continue. He glanced over his shoulder and knew the soldiers listened in. "My most fervent wish would be for you not to become further involved, for I am already lost."

"You must not say such things," she protested.

"Time's up," one of the soldiers announced.

"Sweet Larissa, give me a kiss and bid me farewell."

Larissa stood on tiptoe and leaned forward to press a kiss upon Sir Randall's lips. In the next instant, a soldier grabbed him by an elbow and dragged him away, preventing their lips from meeting. In a final attempt to touch him, Larissa reached out to stroke his cheek, only to meet with emptiness.

Robbed of her kiss, Randall gave up hope he would ever set eyes on her again. "Wills, take care of her," he called out over his shoulder, trudging between the guards through the foyer. His moist gaze met hers for a fleeting moment before he was pulled out of the house.

William caught Larissa, preventing her from watching Randall board the prison transport. He was glad she would be spared from that humiliation.

Larissa hated how Sir Randall had been pulled from her, and it infuriated her that he had been placed in this predicament. What was she going to do? "Where will they take him?"

"To prison." Lord William placed a sympathetic arm around her, leading her away from the others for the privacy of the parlor and closed the doors.

"He didn't do it! He didn't!" Larissa professed in quiet anguish.

"I know he didn't," Lord William agreed, when well out of earshot from the others.

Larissa twisted out from under Lord William's arm to face him. "We have to help him. We have to discover who did this to him." She grabbed his jacket and shook him. There was no one else who would help her. No one she could trust. Lord William believed in Sir Randall's innocence as much as she did. He just couldn't refuse her. He couldn't. "You have to help me. You must!" she cried in desperation.

"Of course, Larissa. I will help you," Lord William replied with calm composure. "Please sit and try to calm down."

The rattle of the tea cart grew louder, nearing.

"Would you care for something stronger than tea? Sherry?"

"No. Tea will be fine." But she didn't want even that. It was all she could do to keep a civilized head. Larissa did not know where to start, or how to go about an investigation. Hopefully, Lord William would have an idea.

After emptying her cup, she lurched to her feet and made a dart across the room, feeling the need to move about. "Where shall we begin?"

"I think we should first question motive." Lord William leaned back in his chair and crossed his legs. "Who would want revenge against him."

"He did not have any enemies that I know of," she offered, wringing the silk handkerchief she had used to dry her tears.

"He had made one recently, I believe . . ." Lord William's voice trailed off.

Larissa came to a standstill behind the sofa, bracing her arms on the back, riveted in complete attention. "Who is it?"

He hesitated. "I do not think I should make hasty accusations." Larissa gave him a hard look, hoping to convince him to tell what he knew. "However . . ."

Lady Brookhurst's shrill voice carried through the house. "I will not stay here a moment longer! This has gone quite beyond the pale, Dorothea."

"Maman, we cannot just up and leave," Dorothea's softer voice followed.

"We can do just that." The groan of the risers told of Lady Brookhurst's mounting the stairs, with the light tread of Dorothea behind. "Now, I'm going to tell Regina to begin packing our things at once. At once, I say, and we'll leave this wretched place."

Lord William reported to Larissa an hour later. "Lady Dorothea and her mother are packing up and leaving for London."

"Do you know why?" she asked.

"It seems Lady Brookhurst has taken offense to my brother's involvement in Sir Randall's arrest. Terrance was quite taken with Dorothea." Lord William paused. "However, if revenge is what she was after, then there is no reason for her to remain."

"Revenge? Dorothea? Whatever do you mean?"

"From what I understand, Randall paid particular attention to Dorothea. Almost as if—" Lord William appeared reluctant to continue, but did so. "As if his intentions were toward marriage. But that was of course until it was discovered you two were already wed."

"I find it very difficult to believe Dorothea capable of such a thing." Larissa thought Dorothea had been so kind not to harbor any bad feelings. Perhaps she had been too willing.

"Oh, she's capable, all right." There was no question of doubt in his voice. "She has quite a reputation."

"If she has such a reputation then why did Sir Randall, or for that matter your own brother, become involved with her?"

"My brother is blinded by Dorothea's beauty, polish, and good manners. As for Randall, I cannot say."

Larissa was glad he did not elaborate about Sir Randall's experience with the ladies and tried to keep focused on the problem of freeing him from prison.

"If we could just speak to him, perhaps he would know why she would wish to do this."

"No. I cannot allow you to set foot near Newgate. Under no circumstances would he ever want you there."

"We must do something." Then it occurred to her. "Dorothea could not have done this alone. She must have had an accomplice, someone to pose as Bussin' Billy."

"It could be almost anyone."

"It was a man, of that I'm sure." The beginnings of a plan began to form in her mind. "If an impostor has been instrumental in condemning Sir Randall, perhaps an impostor can help vindicate him as well."

"What exactly do you have in mind?" Lord William gave Larissa a most peculiar look.

"We must return at once to London," she announced.

"And see if we can persuade Lady Dorothea to aid us without her realizing."

A few hours later, Larissa waited in the foyer with her bonnet in place, her green traveling cloak fastened, and her bandbox in hand. The solitary thought that repeated in her mind was, *The sooner we leave, the sooner we get there.*

"Are you ready, then?" Lord William inquired several minutes later when he arrived.

Larissa nodded and hurried to the front door without waiting. "We must be on our way."

"Where the devil are you going?" Lord Melton shouted, striding into the foyer. He appeared more short-tempered than usual. "William!"

Larissa stiffened. The marquess was indeed in ill temper. Lord William remained calm and responded. "I am seeing Lady Trent back to London."

Melton grumbled to himself and glanced from his brother to Larissa, considering his judgment on the matter.

"Terrance, surely you can see Lady Trent cannot remain here. Sir Randall has entrusted her well-being to me. I must see her safely to Rushton House," Lord William explained.

The fact was all the other guests had gone. With Larissa and Lord William leaving, Melton would indeed be all alone in his monstrosity of a house. It appeared he was suffering and did not intend to suffer alone. Larissa thought in his present condition the marquess should not inflict himself upon others. He was not fit to share company with anyone.

"Oh, all right," Melton blustered. "But I expect you to return at once. Do you hear?"

With his brother's blessing, Lord William hurried Larissa outside to the waiting coach. He signaled for the driver to be off to their destination. By the time they arrived, Larissa intended to have a feasible plan to set into motion.

Lord William sat on the opposite bench from her. It did not take more than a few moments before his body began to slouch in the seat and his head lowered onto his chest as sleep overtook him.

"Oh, do stay awake." Larissa prodded him.

"Awfully sorry," he apologized. "It's a bad habit." He readjusted himself so he sat upright, making a discernible effort to remain alert. "Where shall we begin? Ah, yes. Think back to last night," he prompted. "I'm certain whatever you can remember about last night will be quite helpful."

"Yes, you're right. I must concentrate and recall every detail of the robbery. There must be some hint that would lead us to Bussin' Billy's identity."

"Was there something someone said or did, anything peculiar that happened at the ball?"

Larissa clasped her hands together, setting them in her lap, and leaned back against the squabs, taking a few minutes and staring at some nonexistent point.

"All right, if nothing comes to mind, what about the robbery itself?"

Larissa sighed. "The evening was warm. We took the curricle."

"The curricle? Dashed bad form. Can't imagine Randall would suggest such an abominable thing."

"He didn't. It was Lord Melton who suggested it. He said it didn't matter. That this was only a country affair."

He leaned closer to her and his voice softened to a whisper. "I think the real reason was he wanted to be alone with Lady Dorothea."

Larissa ignored Lord William's last statement and concentrated on his first. "It *was* warm that night, wasn't it? Did Lord Melton not say Dorothea had the pistol in a fur muff?"

"Why would she carry a muff?"

"I want to know *why* she would carry a pistol." Larissa looked up at Lord William, considering hers the more important of the two questions.

Chapter Twenty-five

She knew. Dorothea must have at least known of, if not orchestrated the robbery herself.

The hour was late when the carriage rolled into Town. Larissa and Lord William had only just arrived and had not yet had a chance to sit when Laurie appeared, announcing Lord Fenton Harding's arrival.

"By all means, Laurie, show Lord Fenton in," Larissa responded.

"Harding? Whatever is he doing here?" Lord William mused, taking up a crystal tumbler and heading for the liquor decanters.

"We'll never find out unless we ask him, will we?" She removed the glass from Lord William's grasp and pointed to the doorway to an adjoining room. "You'd better get out of sight, or all our plans will be ruined."

"Me, hide?" he cried, half taken by surprise and half insulted. "How undignified."

"Better undignified than discovered. Go on now." She gave him an encouraging push in the direction of the side door. William reclaimed his glass and snagged the brandy decanter before making his exit.

Larissa settled on the sofa, looking calm and manageable, since she didn't know what to expect from her guest.

Lord Fenton bounded up the stairs, fairly running to Larissa's side. He settled next to her and took her hand, lending comfort. "I heard the terrible news. I came as soon as I could," Lord Fenton said this without a trace of the temper he had displayed on the day of the barge party.

"If you had arrived any sooner, you would have been here before me."

"I hope you are not making jokes at a time like this," he replied in all seriousness.

"I am sorry. I am feeling rather fatigued."

"It is I who should be sorry. How inconsiderate of me to overlook your comfort."

"I appreciate your efforts, Lord Fenton."

"Please, I do wish you would call me Fenton."

She smiled. "Fenton, then."

"I want you to know I shall be here if you should need me."

"How very kind of you." Larissa found she almost could forget his momentary burst of anger, as if it had been a dream that she had long ago.

"He didn't deserve you," Fenton whispered. "Sir Randall was not at all as attentive to you as a husband should be. He carried on despicably with other women right under your nose. I cannot imagine that you would ever have tolerated his vulgar behavior."

"I did not find his behavior suspect in any case," she replied.

"You cannot deny, you in turn sought solace from another quarter." He made it sound like an accusation.

"Well, I . . ." Larissa found it quite impossible to refute. How else would it appear when one saw her situation through his eyes?

"Regardless of your past circumstance and because of our prior association, I wish you to know I shall be entirely at your disposal. I beg you, do not hesitate to depend on me."

After kissing her hand in farewell, Fenton drew her into a warm embrace. She could feel herself tremble within the solidness of his arms.

"Remember, my dear Larissa," he whispered against her hair, "I shall be here for you." He released her and strode off, pausing at the top of the stairs to glance back at her as if to assure her of his stoic resolve.

"What do you think of all that?" Lord William drawled. He emerged from his hiding place, holding an open decanter and stopper in one hand and his half-filled glass in the other.

"I'm not entirely sure," Larissa replied, drooping into a thoughtful repose.

Lord William finished his drink and refilled his glass. With a practiced single motion he set the near-empty container on the sideboard and replaced the stopper.

The next morning, Larissa made straight for the Brookhurst residence on Green Street.

Waiting in the morning room, Larissa gathered all the

warmth and kindness she could manage to present a genuine display. The success of the plan depended upon how well she could convince Lady Dorothea of her sincerity. This would be the performance of a lifetime.

"How kind of you to receive me," Larissa offered with a warm smile.

"Think nothing of it, Lady Trent," Dorothea said in a kind and understanding lilt.

"Please, you must not hold with formalities," she begged. "At Carswell Castle, you called me Larissa."

"Yes, of course, *Larissa.* I feel sympathetic with your plight. The only marginally less scandalous thing that occurred was Lord Melton turning in Sir Randall. I'll never be able to forgive him for that." She gave an exasperated sigh. "My only distress is that I could have been interested in him." Dorothea's gaze darted back to Larissa. "I refer to Lord Melton, of course. I do not for one minute believe Sir Randall is Bussin' Billy."

"Of course not. I know you believe in him as much as I do." Larissa watched Dorothea's expression. "You've been the kindest friend. That's why I came to see you myself to give you the good news."

"Good news?" Dorothea's interest was piqued.

Larissa gave an exhilarated smile. "Sir Randall is being released. They've caught the real Bussin' Billy."

"Released?" Dorothea looked suitably shocked and stammered, "H-how? W-why?"

"I am so very relieved," Larissa sighed.

"How fortunate for you and for him as well." Dorothea added, "I can see that he loves you very much."

"Can you?" Larissa prompted for conversation's sake.

There were times she had detected a genuine look of adoration in Sir Randall's eyes.

"It is unmistakable." Dorothea's tone flattened, at odds with her usual musical inflections. It sounded as if she were quite envious.

A scant half hour later, Larissa boarded the carriage and traveled down the street, turning the corner away from the townhouse. She called to the driver to stop and leaped out. She ran back toward the house to find Lord William watching the house she had just left.

"How did it go? Do you think she believed you?" Lord William kept his eyes focused on the front of the residence.

"I think so," Larissa said. "I *hope* so."

"Then she should be making her move soon. Why don't you go back to Rushton House and I'll meet you there when all this is over."

"I hope you'll have good news."

"I hope so too." Lord William sighed. "Now, go on before we are both discovered."

Larissa rushed back to the waiting carriage and reboarded. It continued down the street toward Portman Square.

Larissa paced in front of the blazing hearth in the drawing room, unable to read or to hold a hoop and needle steady to embroider. For the hundredth time, she spun her skirts around her legs to change direction. It had been more than two hours. Yes, two hours, she confirmed when she glanced at the mantle clock. How much longer could this possibly take?

The sound of footfalls ascending the staircase. Finally

Lord William had returned. She wrung her hands with impatience, anxious to hear of his findings.

"Larissa, my dear!" The voice of Lady Rushton echoed from the stairs. She greeted her niece with wide open arms.

"Aunt Ivy?" Larissa squeaked out, bearing her aunt's embrace. Lord Rushton joined them only moments later. She felt more shocked than relieved at their unexpected arrival. "You've returned early."

"Your aunt had the most frightful notion that some terrible fate had befallen you or some such thing." Rushton gave a hearty laugh and strolled past them into the drawing room. Ivy followed, leading Larissa by the hand.

"You see, my dear, your niece is fine." Rushton moved to the sideboard and poured himself a brandy.

Larissa kept quiet, unnaturally so.

"If all is well, then I believe I shall take the opportunity to rest a bit. It was such a long trip and I was in such a hurry to come home and see you." On her way out, Ivy pressed Rushton's hand. "I apologize for causing you to race home."

"Do not give it another thought, my angel. I am only too glad to comply with your every wish." Rushton smiled and kissed her cheek.

Ivy smiled and gave a wistful sigh. "I fear I am more fatigued than I thought. I shall see you at dinner, my dear." She turned to Larissa before leaving. "Have you done something different with your hair? In any case, it looks lovely."

Rushton waited until Ivy had climbed up the next set of stairs before asking, "Pray tell, where is my nephew?"

"My lord," Larissa began, sinking into the sofa to face him. "I fear there *is* bad news."

"My nephew again, is it?" By the tone of Rushton's voice, she suspected the earl already knew the answer even as he asked the question.

Larissa fortified herself to make the explanation. She knew he wouldn't be at all pleased. Before she could reply, Lord William entered.

"My word—William Felgate!" Rushton spouted.

"Lord Rushton. . . ." Lord William blustered, equally surprised.

"He and my aunt have just this minute returned," Larissa informed him. "The earl is asking about Sir Randall."

"Randall. . . . Have you told him?" Lord William's already grim expression became more so. "The news is most grave."

"How bad can it be?" Rushton sat in a chair, remaining unconcerned for the most part. "Randall is one of those lads whose behavior rivals a saint's."

"Not this time, I'm afraid."

Rushton returned a hard stare at Lord William. "I'll have your hide if you've had a hand in this."

"My lord, Lord William has been most kind and is doing everything he can to help Sir Randall from his unfortunate predicament."

"Help?" Rushton looked from Lord William to Larissa and back again, narrowing his eyes. "What kind of trouble is the lad in?"

Larissa and Lord William exchanged glances, a silent

interaction of who would relay the tale to the earl of his nephew's fate. Lord William's look told her if she couldn't do it, he would take on the responsibility and the violent reaction that was sure to follow.

"My lord, I regret to inform you Sir Randall is presently incarcerated," Lord William bravely stated.

"Prison!" The brandy sloshed out of Rushton's snifter when he bolted upright.

"He has been arrested for robberies under the identity of the highwayman known as Bussin' Billy."

"Robbery!" Rushton snorted in outrage. "This is preposterous. I'd stake my title on his innocence."

"We are fully convinced of that as well," Larissa concurred.

"We're trying to discover who did this horrid thing," Lord William continued.

"Do you know?" the earl questioned.

"We have our suspicions." Again, Lord William and Larissa exchanged looks. "But the evidence against Sir Randall is irrefutable."

"But still circumstantial," Larissa added in a ray of hope.

"Speaking of evidence," Lord William began, "I've managed to recover my brother's family crested ring and matching stickpin."

Rushton arched a brow, giving a suspicious glare. "And how exactly did you come by this stroke of good luck?"

"I made a point of checking some pawnshops in hopes of retrieving further clues."

" 'Pon my oath, my nephew had no part in this. Someone

has framed him. Who do you think is responsible for this outrage?"

"Lady Dorothea Brookhurst," Larissa enunciated each syllable in a concise tone. She went on to explain the further details of how it came to be that she and Sir Randall accepted the invitation of Lord William after their secret marriage had been discovered.

Then she explained how the arrival of Melton and his party changed the laconic country stay into the beginning of tirade of thieves by the highwayman Bussin' Billy. How the thief's torn greatcoat and muddy boots planted in Sir Randall's wardrobe at Carswell Castle were discovered after the Bow Street Runners were called in. The gunshot wound he incurred the same night as Bussin' Billy convinced the earl of the intricacy of the plot.

After Larissa had finished, Rushton sat silent for several minutes. "I see" is all the earl said, taking a brief pause. "And precisely how did you think to free my nephew?"

"We thought if we could convince Dorothea he had already been released, she would have her accomplice appear again as Bussin' Billy to reimplicate Sir Randall. If Billy were to strike while Randall were in jail, the authorities would have no choice but to release him."

"Speaking of accomplices," Lord William spoke, "I followed our bird to Albemarle Street."

"Grillion's?" Rushton wondered and Lord William nodded.

Larissa shook her head. The name did not mean anything to her.

"It's a fashionable hotel where single gentlemen stay," Lord William explained.

"That doesn't tell us any more than we already know," Larissa said. She had hoped something more would be learned by following Dorothea.

"If we were to capture the highwayman"—Rushton went further to postulate—"we could solve this puzzle once and for all."

Rushton eased back into his chair.

"It's time to move on to stage two," Lord William advised.

"And what would that be?" Rushton inquired.

"To parade the newly released Sir Randall about town," Lord William declared. "By donning his clothes, darkening my hair and escorting my friend's new wife about town, I believe I can successfully convince the citizens of our fair city I am Sir Randall Trent." Lord William gave a gracious bow in an imitation of the baronet's finest.

Rushton pursed his lips and nodded his approval. "Yes, I think it just might work."

"I think it's a stroke of genius," Lord William praised.

"One of your schemes, is it? More sound than the ones you usually come up with."

"I have to be honest. It is one of Lady Trent's."

"Yes, *Lady Trent,* indeed." Rushton regarded her with raised eyebrows. Larissa forced a smile and took the credit, but wondered what rampant thought fueled the earl's questioning gaze.

That very afternoon, Larissa and a disguised Lord William traveled to Hyde Park. Riding in the earl's crested coach lent credence to their performance. The coach stopped, allowing its passengers to disembark and stroll along the path. Larissa took the inside track. Her escort's back faced the approaching pedestrians. From behind, one would assume the dark-haired gentleman under the curly-brimmed hat and fawn coat with velvet lapels would be her husband, Sir Randall Trent.

Larissa used her parasol to shield Lord William's face from recognition. Alternately, Lord William used his hat to mask his identity when the parasol could not. They thought to keep their distance from the rest of the throng yet greet those on foot as well as those in passing transports openly.

Talk of their presence would soon be widespread and get back to Dorothea, hopefully to spur her into action. After a very public disclosure of marriage and the sudden news of Sir Randall's arrest, the rumor of his release should be seized with equal enthusiasm.

After the stroll, Larissa and Lord William met up with their coach. Larissa knew the only way to be rid of the surreptitious glances and intrusive stares from the onlookers would be when the coach rounded the corner and pulled out of the line of sight of the public. Until then they were onstage.

"Did you see the look on Mrs. Peacock's face?" Larissa whispered, approaching the coach.

"Can't say I did," he mumbled.

"She looked as though she had seen a ghost. And Lady Jersey looked absolutely stupefied." Larissa made her final visual sweep of the area. "They saw who they wanted to see. I'm sure the news will be spread within the hour."

"Dash it all," he swore. "I had my back to everyone. I couldn't see a blessed thing."

The liveried footman opened the door. Before handing Larissa up, Lord William delivered a smart slap to her derrière. She gave a sharp cry, leaping into the transport.

Larissa kept silent, only glaring at him until the coach moved off. "What did you do that for?" It was all she could do not to rub the assaulted area.

Lord William sat on the opposite bench, facing her. "Harding said Randall wasn't a gentleman, that he treated you badly and all that. I was just throwing myself into the part."

"Well, you can just throw yourself out," Larissa huffed. "Nothing could be further from the truth. Sir Randall was a consummate gentleman." Unless she counted the steamy gazes followed by the sensual half smile he effected while in her presence.

She did not want to admit she might never experience another moment of his company. Yet, it might happen if Sir Randall were to be found guilty.

"It was meant as a love pat, an endearment, that's all," Lord William continued.

"I'll ask you not to repeat that endearment, thank you."

"As you say." Lord William leaned forward and doffed his hat as an apology, causing the sound of tearing fabric to fill the interior.

Larissa could see the fabric of the jacket strain across the shoulders. Lord William's arms were held tight. A slight shift to his right side provided Larissa a view of the ruptured shoulder seam. He tried to look for himself, but could not quite see.

"Oh, goodness," Larissa whispered.

"Oh, bloody hell," he swore. "This is Randall's favorite coat. I'll have the devil to pay when he finds out." His eyes softened when he met Larissa's gaze. "But I would gladly take the thrashing if our scheme works."

Chapter Twenty-six

"Y̶ou didn't expect Billy to charge out and take action right away, did you?" William inquired the following evening.

Larissa wrung her lace handkerchief. "How much longer do you think it will be?"

"Can't say really. It was only yesterday the two of you paraded through Hyde Park," Rushton remarked. "The impostor must strike soon if they are to keep up the pretense that my nephew is the highwayman."

"I don't know what I expected. It just feels like we've been waiting forever."

"Waiting is such a terrible business," William agreed, downing his brandy and immediately refilling it. "Can't do a blessed thing but sit here all the while. I don't know how much more I can take myself."

"Don't know if my cellar will last," the earl remarked, commenting on his guest's brandy consumption.

Dressed to the nines, Ivy breezed into the room. "I'm sorry to keep you waiting, Rushton."

"And worth every extra minute, I'll wager." Rushton reached out for his wife's hand and eyed her thoroughly. Emeralds and diamonds glittered from her ears, throat, and wrists. "You are an absolute vision, my sweet."

"Rushton," she whispered, chiding him. Her dark green dress rustled when she stepped back. "Do stop."

"We shall be off to do our part," the earl announced. "I'll see what tidbits of news I can gather tonight. Perhaps if we're lucky one of the guests will have had the horrible tragedy of an unexpected meeting with the highwayman."

"No need to sound so jubilant about someone else's misfortune," the countess scolded. "If we don't leave now, Rushton, we'll be more than fashionably late."

"I'm coming, I'm coming, my dear. No need to threaten to leave me behind."

"I never said I would leave without you."

"You haven't yet," Rushton said, producing a teasing smile. He made a final farewell gesture to Larissa and William.

William raised his glass in a toast. The Earl and Countess of Rushton left. William took the empty decanter to the sideboard and searched for a full bottle. "Why don't you take yourself off to bed."

Larissa resumed her pacing. "I do not think I shall be able to face sleep until they return."

Unable to find his drink of choice, William found a substitute, filled his glass, and sank into the wingback chair next to the fire. He stretched, then crossed his legs at the ankles and rolled his glass between his palms. "All I can say is we had both better prepare ourselves for a very long evening."

Three hours later, Larissa heard the steady sound of footsteps approach the parlor. William's, she thought, or perhaps Laurie's. She froze with her needle poised in hand when she looked up and saw Sir Randall standing in the doorway.

The embroidery hoop slipped from her fingers and fell off her lap. She rushed toward him, but stopped just beyond arm's reach. "You're back," she gasped with suppressed pleasure, an exuberant smile, and her heart nearly pounding out of her chest in excitement.

"I have a hard time believing it myself." His voice sounded as gritty as his rumpled and torn clothing. A dark wash of whiskers covered his chin, causing the dark circles under his eyes to stand out on his drawn, gaunt face. "They told me they had the wrong man and I was free to return home."

"Good Gad! I can't believe it, you're back!" William approached his friend from behind and clapped both hands on Sir Randall's shoulders in welcome. He immediately withdrew them, leaning away and brushing them together as if soiled. "You look a fright and you smell worse."

"As bad as I feel, no doubt," Sir Randall groaned.

William carved a judicious path around his friend, entering the room to stand next to Larissa. "Here now, Randall. You're no fit sight for a lady."

Sir Randall looked down at himself. Did he not know of his own condition?

"Your bath awaits, sir," Laurie announced from out of nowhere.

Sir Randall gave a brief nod, excusing himself. Laurie followed. In the silence that ensued, Larissa could hear the butler continuing his discourse. "The cook is preparing your meal now, sir. It should be ready by the time you finish."

"Laurie, I can't ever remember when I've been so hungry. I didn't think I'd ever taste Amendola's fare again."

When Sir Randall was well out of sight, William gave a leap, clicking his heels in midair. "We did it!" he shouted. "At first I thought that plan of yours was fairly half-baked. But it certainly did set things to rights."

"You never told me you thought it unsound."

"I didn't have anything better to suggest," William confessed. "What a sight, what?" His brows wrinkled. "Can't imagine what it would have been like to be in such a place."

Larissa tilted her head, unable to discern his meaning.

"He wasn't in the debtor's side, you know." He rubbed his chin in a contemplative gesture. "Randall's been in with the murderers, thieves, and cutthroats."

"How horrible. How very horrible for him." She shuddered. "Hopefully all of it will soon be forgotten. All that matters now is that he is back where he belongs."

Randall could hardly believe he was safe in his uncle's house. Soaking in the heated water of his bath, he scrubbed at the dirty layer of prison that accompanied him home. He hoped the experience of the dark, dank communal cell he occupied would soon be forgotten.

During his incarceration, bouts of doubt and hopelessness had weaved their way into his mind. He could not move past the notion that he was a lost cause and beyond help.

The days had passed. Just as he had given up all hope, he was set free. He did not know how it came about, or who he could thank for this miracle, but decided chances were good the person or persons responsible resided in this house.

The realization of freedom dawned on him when he stepped onto the brick walk of the Portman Square townhouse, the most wonderful sight in the world.

Satisfied with his exterior, he was ready to abandon his bath and move on to his internal needs. The rumblings of his stomach were causing white caps to form on the water.

Randall feasted on Amendola's reheated culinary masterpiece, and would never have complained of it in a hundred years. The roasted beef and vegetables were a feast compared to the slops they called food at the prison. Satisfied with his solitude, he had no doubt Larissa or the countess would have scolded him on his table manners. He ate like a starving man. He *was* a starving man.

He had come to realize he loved Larissa. Their unfulfilled scene, tragic in its outcome, lay unresolved in his heart. It was the solitary thought that had cut through his blackness and desperation to give him hope. Randall had been given a second chance at life and he did not want to spend the rest of it without her.

In the parlor, William caught Larissa staring over his shoulder to Sir Randall, who stood at the portal.

"I say, there you are," drawled William, turning about to see his friend. "So much better, don't you think?" he asked Larissa.

The absence of her reply drew William's attention. Randall's gaze was locked on her, and hers, in return, on him.

William cleared his throat, but it did not break the spell.

"Well," William glanced between the two and stood. "I suppose I should be leaving you two alone."

Silence.

"I've sent off a note to your uncle of Randall's release. He's attending the Devonshire's musicale." William paused. "I know he'd want to know you were home safe and sound."

Silence still.

"I'll just be on my way then, if you don't mind." William rolled up onto the balls of his feet and swung his arms forward, slapping his fist with an open hand, making a popping sound. "I'll just be in my room if I am needed." He pointed out the door to the stairs, indicating his impending exit. "*So* good to have you back, Randall," he reiterated, noting Randall was not paying the least bit of attention to him and made a hasty retreat.

"Do you know who is responsible for my freedom?"

"I imagine that would be me," Larissa gladly confessed.

"You?" Clearly the news shocked him. "Would you care to explain?"

Feeling a bit self-conscious, she continued, "We couldn't just let them take you away to prison. You are innocent."

"*I* knew that. I'm greatly relieved you so soundly believe it."

"Of course I do. We all did," she was quick to amend. "It was a simple matter of deducing who would want to see harm come to you."

"I fancy I haven't that many enemies," he replied, apparently curious, but not overanxious to discover the culprit. "And who, pray tell, did you come up with?"

"Lady Dorothea Brookhurst."

"Lady Dorothea? Are you quite certain?"

"Oh yes," she nodded. "However, there is little we know about her accomplice, except it is a man. Your uncle was very quick to accuse. He even suspected William of having a part in all this."

"*William?*" Sir Randall pronounced in a peculiar tone. "That's ridiculous. When was it you omitted using his title?"

"Well, I suppose our familiarity has come from our combined efforts to save you. We have been through much together these last few days." She lowered her gaze.

"There's nothing between the two of you is there?" His tone indicated his wariness.

"Other than friendship, no. He has assisted me in having your neckcloths replaced, and he has been impersonating you while you were . . . away."

"Has he now?" Randall inched forward, closing the distance between them. "And while posing as me, has he taken any liberties he should not have?"

"Well," Larissa hesitated. "He had to be convincing in

portraying you. And he couldn't let anyone see his face, of course."

"Of course." The more curious Randall grew, the wider his eyes became. "Is there anything else?"

"There was one particular incident." She paused and swallowed hard. "I'm afraid he . . . I'm not at all sure I should tell you."

"I think you should," he urged. Had Wills behaved improperly toward her? Had he found favor with her, replacing him?

"Well, if you insist." Larissa's large green eyes stared up at him. "I'm afraid he has torn your fawn jacket, the one with the velvet lapels." It appeared she was more concerned about his apparel than the fact she was on first-name basis with *his* friend.

"I am certain it can be easily repaired. It's just your clothes were a touch snug on him. I promise I shall repair it myself, if you like."

"I don't care a fig about the jacket. Larissa," he gasped, snatching up her hand and kissing it. "While I was locked up, I could think of nothing but you. Have you missed me half as much as I have missed you?" He kissed her hand again. "Do you long for the kiss we were denied when I was taken away?"

Her silence and the rising color in her cheeks gave him his answer.

"I never want to leave you again."

She said nothing and remained quiet, giving the indication of submission. Leaning forward, Randall closed the distance between them and took her chin lightly between his fingertips. Her breath felt warm and sweet upon his newly shaved skin. He traced the curve of her lips with his finger before nearing for a kiss. He closed his eyes and leaned toward her.

This was the moment he had long awaited.

Chapter Twenty-seven

The parlor doors flew open. Larissa and Randall leaped apart.

The Earl of Rushton coursed into the room. "Good to have you home, lad!" Tears formed in the earl's eyes and he pulled his nephew into his arms for a quick embrace. "And I believe felicitations are also in order! How you managed to legshackle yourself so quickly is beyond me. I am certain it was due to my influence. I have no doubt you must have married her because you truly love her." He nudged Randall and winked.

Randall opened his mouth to respond, but nothing came out.

"I thought I heard strange voices." William appeared at the door.

"Congratulations on your success." Rushton reached for his hand and shook it. That was a first. Uncle Cyrus had never been fond of William. Up until now, he was considered a young man with disposable income and idle time on his hands who would someday lead Randall into trouble. "Tonight I heard of the highwayman's antics. It was the Duke of Bedford he held up last night and who knows who it will be tonight."

"Tonight?" Larissa repeated. "Why should he strike tonight?"

"Why should he stop?" Rushton asked. "What if this insane vendetta of Dorothea's continues and she persists in seeing you to the gallows?"

"You know, Uncle, I hadn't thought of that."

"Well, you'd better think of it. It's not just your life we're talking about. You've a wife now and you must think of her as well."

"Ah, yes, my *wife*," Randall stammered. His gaze skittered to Larissa.

"If the authorities found the stolen items in your possession, there would not be any question of your guilt," Rushton pointed out.

"Need we prove Lady Dorothea's involvement? After all, aside from the stolen items, no one was hurt," Larissa said.

"No one was hurt?" Randall remarked. "What do you call this?" He rubbed his arm.

"I refer to anyone save you. After all, you are the one around whom the revenge is centered."

"Am I to blame for Lady Dorothea's derangement?"

"Come now, you must have done something to deserve her wrath," William replied.

Randall paused, giving the matter some thought. "I can't say I harmed her in any way, certainly not intentionally.

However, we did have what you might call a misunderstanding." The stares surrounding him begged him to continue. "She wanted me to offer for her."

"Ha! That's rich, you're already wed." Rushton guffawed. "That may just be where the difficulty lies."

"No man would be in his right mind to marry her," William replied without hesitation. "You've been away the past several years, my friend. You do not know of her reputation."

No man's safe with her. She'll wind a man around her little finger and grab hold of him by his vitals.

"If your uncle is correct in assuming Dorothea will persist, what can we do?" It was good to see William was not about to abandon him.

"I want you to go on impersonating me."

"If I am you," William began. "Then you are . . ."

"Free to investigate," Randall stated. "Why don't we see if we can help her along. We should make the situation as tempting as possible."

"What are you about, lad?" Rushton asked.

"A judicious word spoken to Lady Dorothea regarding my uncle's dismay of my circumstance. And to further suggest an unwillingness to come to my aid if such an accusation should be leveled a second time might prompt her to take action, thinking she might succeed."

William now saw the answer to his friend's predicament. "If we could catch her accomplice we could see to their arrest and the end of your troubles."

"Arrest might not be necessary," Rushton pointed out.

"What?" William balked. "Hang the lot of them, I say."

"If the two parties were caught, shall I say, in the act,"

Rushton enlightened the others, "threatened by their impending arrest, they might be convinced to leave the country."

They all nodded, understanding the earl's reasoning.

The countess swept into the room. "Sir Randall, there you are—free at last!" She offered him her gloved hand. "And married to my dear, darling niece." She turned to Larissa. "Why did you not tell me?"

Rushton gave a cough. "He's been occupied elsewhere, my dear," he said, saving Randall from an awkward, lengthy, and completely fictitious explanation. "All will be explained in due time."

Ivy startled when she saw Larissa. "It is nearly two in the morning. Why have you not gone to bed? You can tell me all about how he swept you off your feet later."

"Sir Randall has just—" Larissa began.

"My only niece married!" Ivy held up a hand. "But I imagine what you have to say to him can wait until the morning. It is so very late. I know you are newly wed just as I am but we ladies must get our rest. Let us be off to bed. Say good night to the gentlemen, dear."

Remaining mute, Larissa waved adieu with one hand while her aunt led her from the parlor and up the stairs. She wanted to be part of the planning session she knew would take place once she retired. Like it or not, necessity dictated Larissa would have to wait until morning.

An eager Sir Randall and Lord William met Larissa in the breakfast room. William ushered her to her seat and held her chair while Sir Randall poured her a cup of chocolate and slid it in front of her.

Larissa chuckled at the flurry of activity sweeping about her. It was a shame they were titled gentlemen for they would have made excellent footmen.

Sir Randall returned with a plateful of eggs, sausage, and ham on her right side. Lord William, on her left, arrived with a heaping plate of potatoes, muffins, and toast.

Larissa took a square of toast in one hand, lifted a forkful of eggs in the other and looked between them. "Would you, Sir Randall, have the toast while Lord William consumes the eggs for me?"

The men regarded one another and burst into laughter.

"I do beg your pardon," William apologized. "We are making pests of ourselves."

"*I* would never be so bold as to point that out."

"We must insist you be on your way as soon as possible," Sir Randall explained.

"Have you a plan? Where am I to go? What am I to do?" The smell of food sitting before her grew unappetizing. Her stomach knotted, anticipation gripped her insides.

"You need to pay Lady Dorothea a call this morning before leaving for Rushton Manor."

"You're sending me away? Why?"

"We need to let Dorothea know that, one, I am out of the way so her accomplice can impersonate me without fear of discovery. Two, she will know where to find us, so when she pays us a visit at Rushton Manor she can plant my uncle's stolen items. Three, she will be certain that when it is discovered, he will never lift a finger to save me."

"Do you think she will believe me?"

"It remains to be seen. But we do need you to set the wheels into motion."

Within the hour, Larissa was on her way to Lady Dorothea's.

"I am always so very happy to see you," Dorothea welcomed. "But whatever are you doing here?"

Larissa hoped to turn the nervousness she felt to her advantage. How was Dorothea to know her quavering voice stemmed from deception and not anger.

"The Earl of Rushton is sending Sir Randall and me to his country estate in Kent," Larissa began.

"But why must he send you away?"

"Rushton is very displeased with Sir Randall. The robbery accusation has the earl enraged." Larissa began to cry and retrieved a handkerchief from her reticule. "I am sorry that I'm such a watering pot."

"It's quite understandable." Dorothea comforted and edged forward, anxious for Larissa's next words. "Can I get you something?"

"No, I will be quite all right in a moment." Larissa dabbed her eyes and continued, "Sir Randall is titled but not well-off, you know. We still need to depend on Rushton's generosity. The earl thinks it best if he is out of the public eye." In a weak, unconvincing tone she added. "Of course, he doesn't believe Sir Randall is capable of the charge."

"Of course he doesn't," Dorothea echoed.

Larissa pressed her handkerchief to her nose. "I would hate to think of Sir Randall arrested a second time. I have the most horrible feeling Rushton would not come to his aid."

"I cannot imagine one would treat his own relative so cruelly." Dorothea gave a fine imitation of shock and outrage.

"The worst possible scenario would be if by some queer coincidence, it was the earl who had been robbed and Sir Randall blamed. I dread to think what might become of my dear Randall. The earl would never, ever forgive him."

"Yes, that would be quite a tangle, wouldn't it?" Dorothea replied, sounding distant.

"I would not confess this to anyone but you. However, I believe the real reason Rushton is sending us away is so that Sir Randall will not have a chance to get into any more trouble."

Dorothea snapped back to life. "It is probably a very wise decision."

"Do you really think so?" Larissa relaxed into the back of the sofa. "Well, we are to leave this afternoon. My aunt and the earl will be returning to the country the following week. I believe they are attending a dinner party at Lord Lambourne's tonight and a ball next Monday at Lord and Lady Raintree's."

"Maman and I are planning to leave by the end of this week ourselves. I have a thought," Dorothea replied, feigning inspiration. "We'll be passing through Kent on our way home. Would you mind if we paid a call?"

"Not at all." Larissa displayed a grand smile. "I would love it above all things. It should be so very wonderful to see a friendly face amid all this unpleasantness."

"Then I promise, Maman and I shall plan on stopping by."

"I do thank you for your kindness, your friendship, and your staunch support of Sir Randall."

Dorothea walked Larissa to the front door. Larissa paused before leaving.

"Whatever should I do without you?"

"Whatever indeed," Dorothea sighed, with a placating smile.

"Goodbye." Larissa waved before stepping into the coach.

She settled onto the velvet seats and had the most peculiar feeling all their assumptions had been correct. Which would mean Lady Dorothea would make her move tonight.

Chapter Twenty-eight

"My beloved," the earl pleaded. "I cannot allow you to place yourself in such danger."

"Not danger, Rushton, an adventure!" Ivy exclaimed. "Are *you* not placing yourself at the very same risk?"

"But my dear, *I* shall not be harmed. If I were, I could not discover my nephew's guilt and shun him publicly. Never fear, no harm shall come to me. However, I am truly concerned for your safety." He wrapped an arm around her. "I beg you, you must leave with your niece."

How could the countess have refused? It turned out in the end, she could not.

"There's the lady I love." Rushton embraced her, showing his gratitude for her ever sensible ways.

Ivy allowed him to kiss her cheek and pushed him away, still not happy with the arrangements. "But do not think you will always succeed in getting what you want." She shook her finger at him.

The earl turned to Randall now that domestic matters were settled. "We must plan our strategy down to the minute. If we make a mistake, all will be for naught. We must take no chances and we must expect the unexpected. Come, my boy, come," the earl urged.

"But, Uncle . . ." he objected, "I shall only be another minute or two."

"Don't you see, we have no time to waste." Rushton clapped his nephew on the shoulder and urged him on.

Randall glanced back at Larissa and made a gesture of helplessness. Apparently, it had not gone unnoticed.

"There will be time enough for the ladies later."

How Randall had wished he could have just blurted out the truth. On the other hand, he did not want to express his affection for Larissa in a clumsy or careless way. He would need to wait. Wait until this confounded mess was over and done with.

At that moment, he felt he was a sorry excuse for a man.

What a dear, sweet man he was Larissa thought.

Moving to the window, Larissa watched the coach pull away from the drive, and caught a glimpse of Sir Randall's retreating profile.

What a tangle they had managed to get themselves into. Surely if Sir Randall did not clear his name, there could be no future for him or them. It was best he left now.

"As long as we're vacating, I wish to leave instructions to have the parlor repainted." Ivy gestured to the room where they stood. "I believe Rushton has always wanted to have it done. He is forever referring to the parlor as blue"—she gave a hearty chuckle—"and I don't know how you could have not noticed that it is yellow."

"Why, yes of course," Larissa agreed.

"Such an oversight. One I shall remedy before we leave for the country." She sighed. "How ever could he do without me?"

Randall consulted his pocket watch. Two and a half hours had passed since he had assumed his position outside the Brookhurst residence. Uncle Cyrus should have left his house over an hour ago. Assuming the robbery would take place between Rushton's House and Lambourne's, the deed should have already occurred.

The thought that his uncle might have been harmed occurred to him, but he quickly dismissed it. If Rushton could not prosecute Randall, Dorothea's plan would surely fail.

Randall rocked his head from side to side, working the tightness in his neck free. He mumbled a silent prayer for his uncle's safety while keeping an observant eye for Dorothea. Tonight he would see this thing complete and rid himself of that woman, if indeed she were involved. Randall swung around toward the approaching footsteps.

"Relax lad, it's only me."

Randall exhaled. "Uncle, I am greatly relieved to see you in good health."

"Never been better." Rushton thumped on his chest. "Might say the entire experience was invigorating. Caused my pulse to quicken and the old heart to pound, as they say."

"Well? Tell me what happened." Randall wanted to know. "Did Billy strike?"

"Exactly as we expected. I took the crested coach so there was no mistake of my identity," Rushton began. "The knave fired his pistol to bring the coach to a halt. I stepped outside and the ruffian shoved me out of the way and peered into the transport. But of course, as we know, it was empty. He was fierce looking, all right. Dressed all in black, wearing a tricorn and a brace of pistols and carrying a third in his hand.

" 'I fear I must deny you the riches of the countess,' I announced. 'For you'll not find her with me this night.' " Rushton paused and reflected. "It was most odd. He never spoke but gestured with the barrel of his pistol. I offered no resistance and handed over my signet ring, stickpin, fob, and pocket watch."

Rushton lowered his voice to a serious tone. "The signet ring will prove most incriminating. I gave a superb performance, if I do say so myself. I was quite good. I went further to threaten him with, 'If I ever discover who you are, I'll see you swing for this. I'll make certain I have the personal honor of dropping the trapdoor beneath your feet!' "

"Did you recognize him?"

"No, but had I not known otherwise, I could very well be convinced it was you."

That wasn't good news, especially coming from his own uncle.

A coach rounded the corner and stopped in front of the Brookhurst residence. The front door opened and a cloaked figure emerged.

"Uncle Cyrus, our prey is about to flee." Randall moved toward the tethered horses.

"Enough of my tale. Let us see an end to this hoax."

Dorothea boarded the waiting coach. Randall and his uncle followed at a discreet distance. The coach pulled up at the theater. They watched Dorothea enter and followed her inside. Randall easily caught sight of her moving toward the upper level. Grasping his uncle's arm, he headed toward the stairs.

One by one, Randall and the earl peered behind the heavy drapes into the boxes to discern the identity of its occupants.

"Did all go well?" she asked.

Randall recognized the voice of Dorothea Brookhurst. He stationed himself just outside the box and motioned for his uncle to near.

"Couldn't have gone any better," the accomplice said.

Rushton stationed himself on the opposite side of the door.

"You should have heard the old man. He'll have an apoplexy when he discovers it was Trent."

Randall peered in during the silent interval and witnessed a small pouch pass between the seated figures.

"Take these and do your worst."

"After my visit to Rushton Manor there will be no doubt of the highwayman's identity. Randall Trent shall not walk away this time. And I can assure you Larissa will fall into your arms for comfort, if that is what you still want."

"Yes, I still want her," the man sounded adamant. "I've gone this far for her, haven't I?"

Randall and his uncle exchanged questioning gazes. The accomplice not only knew Larissa, but knew her well enough to be in love with her.

At intermission the lights came up. The drapes pulled open, revealing Randall and the Earl of Rushton blocking the exit. Dorothea and Lord Fenton Harding faced them.

"I will be taking what belongs to me if you don't mind Lady Dorothea." Rushton held out his hand.

"I'm sure I don't know what you are talking about." Dorothea sniffed at the indignity.

"Come now, Trent, let us by," Fenton demanded.

"No. I don't think I shall." Randall snatched up Dorothea's reticule and handed it to his uncle for inspection. Reaching for her dress, he rifled through the material.

"What do you think you are doing?" Dorothea protested with a muffled shriek.

"Trying to discern whether you dabble in black magic or if you simply have a black heart." He stilled, finding exactly what he expected. "What have we here?" Within the folds of her dress he removed a pouch from a hidden pocket. Opening the bag he reached in and plucked out a gold signet ring. "I believe this is yours, Uncle."

Rushton stared at the item. "So it is," he commented. "How is it you come to have possession of this, Lady Dorothea? It was stolen by Bussin' Billy this very night."

Dorothea's gaze flew to Fenton.

An easy smile slid onto Rushton's face. "You need not face the gallows or jail, either of you." The earl shifted to gaze upon Dorothea.

"What do you mean?" Fenton sounded scared. He should have been scared. Rushton was not making an idle threat.

"A most convincing performance, Harding," Rushton's voice was more accusing than complimentary. "I commend you on your ability to impersonate my nephew. I might point out *his* mane is naturally dark, not created to appear so."

The earl fingered the ends of Fenton's hair, then held them out to reveal a dark residue.

"This was all your idea!" Fenton shouted in his defense, jabbing an accusing finger at Dorothea.

"Do not say another word," Dorothea warned through clenched teeth with alarming calm.

"I do not need a confession." Rushton's demeanor took on the noble stature of a peer of the realm. "I can stand testament to your guilt."

Rushton stared into Fenton's eyes, verifying recognition.

"I'm not going to the gallows to save you," Fenton exclaimed.

"Shut up, you fool!" she shouted.

"I am a fair man," Rushton stated. "I give you a choice. You have until tomorrow afternoon to leave the country or I shall report you to the authorities myself."

Dorothea's mouth opened in outrage. Randall expected to hear a protest. None came.

"We have cause to celebrate," Rushton proclaimed upon his arrival the following night at Rushton Manor. "Break out the champagne, Watkins!"

"You are back!" Ivy remarked. He pulled Ivy near and planted a kiss on each cheek. "We are just about to sit down to supper."

Randall met with a hardy welcome from William and a reserved greeting from Larissa. "My dear." He bent over her hand and gave it a slight squeeze, then announced,

"We have been successful. My name has been cleared and the culprits have fled!"

The pop of a champagne cork echoed from the hallway.

The earl told of the robbery. In hindsight, Randall realized danger was minimal, yet Uncle Cyrus exaggerated the tale into one that held the utmost drama. Rushton had Ivy, Larissa, and William sitting literally on the edge of their chairs.

Watkins finally arrived with the champagne and circulated through the room, distributing the glasses.

"To all of us!" Rushton raised his glass in a toast. The others chorused the cheer.

"Look." Randall directed Larissa's attention to his glass. "I'd have thought the champagne flat by now, but it has bubbles." It was a jab at how long it had taken the ancient butler to pull the cork and deliver the champagne to the guests.

Larissa gasped at Randall's ill manners. He was not usually rude, but he felt little patience since every moment spent with her had been interrupted.

Rushton had settled next to Ivy on the sofa. After a second glass of champagne, he urged his nephew to finish the tale. Randall recounted the events of the confrontation of Dorothea and Fenton at the theater.

All through supper they discussed and theorized about the two villains. After the meal, Ivy and Larissa left the men to their port. The men did not remain and followed Rushton to the drawing room instead.

"I really should be on my way," William offered, finishing the remainder of his after dinner drink.

"Must you? So soon?" Randall sounded rather anxious and encouraging. Larissa applied her sharp elbow to Randall's ribs, silencing him.

"I'm afraid I must. I have outlived my usefulness and far overstayed my welcome," he explained.

"William, you mustn't think so," Larissa voiced in sympathy.

"Please," he held up his hand. "Just promise me you'll keep this young pup from finding any more trouble."

"I shall do my best." The blush that rose in her cheeks was so very attractive, Randall thought.

Noting he would be rising early to leave for Carswell Castle, William finished his farewells and retired for the night. Randall was grateful beyond measure to his friend and even more indentured to him because he was the first to bed.

Ivy was the next to claim fatigue. No doubt Rushton would follow his wife, leaving Randall and Larissa alone.

"All this is so very exciting," the countess said. "Much too exciting for me." She kissed her niece on the cheek. "I share your happiness on the return of your husband." Addressing Randall she said, "I congratulate you on your newfound freedom." She pressed her cheek to his. At the doorway, the countess spoke to Rushton. "I shall see you presently, I hope." She widened her eyes, giving him a silent order to follow.

"Yes, dear," he agreed. "As you say, presently."

Did this mean Uncle Cyrus was not going with her?

"Come with me, my boy. I want to discuss an increase in your quarterly allowance. Now that you're a married man, no doubt you will want to buy a house and settle down."

"I don't really think now is the best time," Randall said, hampering his uncle as tactfully as he could. It had been an age since he had seen Larissa, and he hadn't the chance for a proper greeting since his arrival. He glanced in her direction and longed to be near her.

"Now's precisely the time," Rushton countered. He wanted to speak to his nephew and Randall knew there was nothing he could say to change his uncle's mind.

His reunion with Larissa would have to wait just a bit longer.

Sitting on the small sofa near the fire in her bedchamber, Larissa leafed through a book when a light rap came from the connecting door. It swung open, revealing a dressing gown-clad Sir Randall.

He strode into the room, a matching sash tied at the waist kept the garment bound, but the open neck exposed part of his smooth chest with just a dusting of dark hair.

"I trust we shan't be disturbed *here,*" he said, sounding as serious as ever.

Larissa closed her book and laid it on her lap, giving him her complete attention.

"It seems every time I get up the nerve to speak my mind, there's a blasted interruption."

"The only one who would dare to invade this sanctum is you," Larissa countered his agitation with calm.

"That's consoling news." He passed in front of her to pace.

"What is it you wish to see me about?"

He swung around to face her. "Do you realize we haven't had a single moment alone since my return?"

"Why do I have the distinct impression you want something from me?"

"Want?" He gave a nervous chuckle, crossing his arms. "I just *want* everything to remain the way it is."

"What exactly do you mean by 'everything?' "

He did not answer her directly, but digressed into an explanation. "We have been kept quite busy"—his voice softened, releasing his discontent and anger—"with exposing Lady Dorothea's collaboration with Lord Fenton in the Bussin' Billy scheme and all. There hasn't been time to attend to much of anything else."

"By 'anything else' you are referring to . . ." she prompted him.

Sir Randall sat next to her and enveloped her hands with his. His dark, soulful eyes gazed at her, making her feel weak and silly. "I don't want our marriage to end."

"But we're not really married." He had been acting this rumor for so long, perhaps he was beginning to believe it himself.

"As far as everyone else is concerned, we've been married since before the Season. Even your aunt and my uncle believe it. We shall never be able to marry openly."

"And you are suggesting what?" Larissa did not need to pretend she did not understand what he was saying, because she didn't.

Sir Randall drew her closer, sliding the sleeve of her wrapper upward to continue his feather-light kisses from her hand up her arm.

"I propose a trip on the Great North Road. Gretna Green, to be specific. To set to right these past few months."

"You want to marry me?" It hadn't come as a surprise, exactly. However, his intentions had caught her off guard.

"You know I am not rich, but I have just been informed that my Aunt Constance, the earl's first wife, my mother's sister, has left an inheritance due to me upon my marriage and my Uncle Cyrus has increased my quarterly allowance threefold. We shall have enough to purchase a house in the country and make modest investments toward our future."

"Do you think I care about money? I would not accept your offer because of money."

"I know," he whispered. "You accept me because of this." Sir Randall pulled her against him and kissed her. When he finally pulled away it left her breathless. He held her close, she could feel his chest rise and fall, fighting for air. "You've told me you wanted me, and I'm telling you I want you. Is that so hard to understand? I can't promise you excitement or adventure."

"Yes, I do love you," she confessed, having an equal problem catching her breath. "I think I have had enough adventures to last a lifetime."

"What I can promise is my love," Sir Randall stated sincerely. "As you wish, no more adventures."

"Nothing would please me more." Larissa met his lips with hers for a slow, wonderful kiss. After all this time of being his rumored wife it would come true, Larissa would become Lady Randall Trent.